PARSE GALAXY BOOK 1

CHAOS ZONE

D1225829

KATE SHEERAN SWED

CHAPTER 1

SLOANE DIDN'T KNOW who had named this place, only that Shard was a poetically appropriate title for a cursed sliver of ground like this one. A leftover from an obliterated planet, Shard had somehow sprouted a city, in the same way that a rock might sprout a diseased fungus.

From a distance, Shard resembled nothing so much as a chunk of eggshell, or a broken piece of pottery. It tipped precariously as it wobbled along its orbit, as if one good hard shove might send it spinning into a neighboring rock.

As bad as it looked from afar, though, Sloane couldn't help feeling that Shard was much, much worse on the ground.

It took the better part of her focus not to lose her footing as she picked her way along the street, stepping around discarded wrappers and mysterious puddles where destroyed fliptabs had just happened to land. Single-use tech, and no doubt stuffed with incriminating data—had the tech not been obviously broken past saving.

It wasn't easy to maintain a don't-talk-to-me swagger while trying not to slip and fall in a puddle of grossness, but

Sloane did her best. She'd been warned away from this place—from the whole Bone System, in fact, by an entire conference table full of Fleet captains—and for good reason. She had to look like she belonged.

Or, at the very least, like she wouldn't make a good mark.

It wasn't that she took the stay-out warning lightly, though she didn't hold much stock in anything a Fleet slug had to say. It was more that she needed tokens—a *lot* of tokens—and she wasn't going to get them by picking up a dish-washing gig.

The power vacuum in the Bone System meant opportunity. And if the Fleet opposed her presence here, well, that was just one more reason to show up anyway.

"Remind me what happened the last time you tried to steal from a casino." Sloane's pilot, Hilda, tiptoed her way along the street a few steps behind, as if hoping Sloane would meet with any unseen traps before she did. She'd wrapped her long gray braid into a bun at the nape of her neck, and she had on a pair of black boots with silver spikes running up the sides. Sloane suspected the boots contained an armory's worth of hidden knives, though she hadn't dared to ask for confirmation.

Hilda piloted Sloane's ship—her uncle's ship, technically—but with no security officer to help, Sloane had had to beg the woman to join her on this job. Shard wasn't the kind of place you landed without someone to watch your back.

"That was a lux casino," Sloane replied. "And I told you, I'm not going to steal."

"What are you going to do, then? Trick? Con? Tap dance?"

Since Hilda wasn't going to like the plan, Sloane opted

to keep her mouth shut. Hilda would understand the job as soon as they reached the casino. Or shortly after.

Assuming they could *find* the casino. Sloane's uncle had abandoned her, it was true, but he'd left behind a treasure trove of information on every underworld ring in the galaxy. Black markets, drug cartels, smuggling rings. If it had a mildly nefarious purpose, Uncle Vin had catalogued it.

But some of her uncle's records were out of date, and things in the Bone System had shifted rapidly since his disappearance. Even if she could find the casino, the entrance protocols might have changed.

If that happened, she'd do what she did best: she'd improvise.

For now, she concentrated on scanning for the casino entrance while also keeping her footing and maintaining the all-important swagger. A hidden casino in a place that was already about as underworld as you could get—at least until you reached the outskirts of the galaxy—was not going to be easy to find.

It was impressive that someone had built a city on Shard at all, even if the effect was more that of a child's tower that'd been made with a pile of rusty blades.

The place was dirty and broken and loud. Every shout echoed down from the dome that enclosed the city, glancing off the repurposed steel beams and layers of scaffolding that somehow seemed to serve as living quarters. Hov-train markers spiraled above the city, the trains themselves obscured behind an orange-tinted cloud of smog and grime. Sloane could hear them, though, the telltale huff-and-grind of their engines cutting through the city noise.

The whole city was a mishmash of jangled music and yells—some happy, some not so—and it smelled moldy and sick, like week-old dishwater. Even the gravity anchors that dotted the pavement to either side were spotted with rust, and Sloane was glad she'd thought to tuck a spare O2 bag into her pocket. If the devices that kept her feet on the ground were that banged up, she didn't want to think about the shoddy maintenance on the life support systems.

The grav anchors looked like dropped coins, as if they could be picked up and shoved into a pocket.

In fact, she was kind of hoping they could.

"There," Hilda said, and Sloane paused, twisting to follow the older woman's extended index finger toward a window with a yellow border. It wasn't the window itself, with its broken pane of glass, or the sickly color of the neon that bordered it; it was the rose petal, a real one, that someone had skewered on the edge of the sill. The bloom was as red as a wound.

"Inviting," Sloane said.

Hilda's fingers twitched, as if she wanted to reach for her boots. "It's not too late to take a bounty instead."

Sloane licked her lips. Maybe Hilda wouldn't object to her plan, after all. Because they *were* here for a bounty. It just... wasn't one Hilda would agree to take.

But their ship wouldn't *make* it to any other bounty. After everything Sloane had put the *Moneymaker* through in the last few months, she'd barely be able to drag it to the closest reputable service station—once she had the money to pay for service—let alone prevail in the inevitable fight that an out-of-atmo bounty hunt would mean.

No, this was the only option. If she said as much to Hilda, though, the pilot might dig her heels in and back right out. So instead, Sloane stepped over a pile of refuse, choosing not to look too closely at it, and sidled up to the door beneath the petal. It looked like every other door on the block, with a slipshod coat of gray paint that was peeling at the corners.

Sloane ran her palm along the stones, searching for a scan point, while Hilda stayed a step behind, arms crossed over her chest. "Try to stop looking like my mother, will you?" Sloane said. "We're here to have fun."

Or pretend to, anyway. But it was more than likely that someone was listening to them by now. No reason to broadcast their plans.

And it *was* probably going to be at least a little fun.

One of the bricks buzzed against her hand, just as Uncle Vin's notes had promised. She said, "Foxglove," and the door clicked open, admitting her into a narrow hall with chipped green paint and a floor that was more rust than metal plating.

According to Vin, the petals outside the window changed regularly—but the password into the place did not. Given that he'd been missing for half a year now, she was lucky the rules hadn't changed.

A second door clapped open, letting Sloane and Hilda slip into a box of an elevator with blue-screen walls, as pleasant as an elevator in a fancy hotel or outlet station.

The car started up, without so much as a shudder, and a light bell tone sounded as if to announce the voice that began to rattle off a welcome. "The seven blades in your boots must be checked."

The voice spoke to them from somewhere in the ceiling, and it issued the instructions in a pleasant, musical voice, even though whatever system could identify and count hidden blades on someone's person was intimidating by default.

The elevator certainly seemed like it belonged to a lux casino. Sloane's father probably didn't even have an elevator this nice back in his penthouse. He definitely didn't have scanning technology that could pick out each individual weapon a person might be carrying.

When Sloane stuck her hand out to prod at the wall, though, her fingers melted straight through a holograph. An open lift. That *was* just like Dad's. Excited, Sloane flicked the holo-walls off, revealing the orange glow of the streets of Shard all around them. The towers looked even more like blades from here, dark and foreboding. This place wasn't pretty. At all.

But the open lift always gave her a rush.

"Don't do that," Hilda said, squeezing her eyes shut. "You're giving me vertigo."

"You're a *pilot*."

"Right. Not an elevator operator."

Sloane didn't want to lose the view, so she dug a fistful of coins out of her pocket. Most places didn't use physical tokens for currency, but she'd brought some along since casinos occasionally did. For fun, she suspected, more than convenience. Who didn't want to see stacks of money adding up on the table?

"Do you know this trick?" she asked.

Hilda was glowering at her. "Where did you even get those coins?"

Not important. Sloane held her hand out, positioning it over the edge of the lift, and dropped the coins, watching as they fell down the channel. They dropped a bit too slowly, as if they'd been caught in a strong breeze.

A count of three later, and the coins were zipping back up toward her, just sparkling glints in the darkness. And they'd multiplied, too; she'd dropped three, and now she counted five.

The coins would ride the channel all the way up to the top of the lift, if she let them.

With a single sweep of her hand, Sloane caught them as they passed the edge of the lift. The take? A pair of rusty gravity anchors from the surface. Not too bad.

"The lift is connected to the grav anchors," Sloane said. "They do that sometimes, when they want to cut corners."

Hilda rolled her eyes. "Excellent. That looks like the kind of trick one could use to, I don't know, heist major amounts of anything magnetic."

Sloane winked. "Exactly."

"I guess I know who taught you how to do that."

And with that, the fun of the game died. Sloane kept the smile on her face, anyway, hoping Hilda couldn't see through it. She'd brought up the trick as a distraction, but she clearly hadn't thought it through. She didn't want to talk about Oliver. Not now, not ever.

Luckily, the elevator voice seemed to have decided that it was time to read the rest of the rules. "Welcome to the Snapdragon. No AIs are allowed. Weapons must be checked. And there is no fighting allowed in the casino, except on Level C."

Sloane would've been willing to bet the voice was tied to some kind of AI, if a limited one, but house rules were house rules.

"Please confirm if you agree," the voice said.

"Confirm," Sloane said. Hilda sighed, then echoed her agreement. Sloane could almost hear her mourning her blades.

Sloane would've liked to promise she'd get them back, but she couldn't. She had three possible exit points in mind, and none of them involved returning through the front door.

The elevator doors opened with a musical cadence, and Sloane stepped out into a dream.

Blue-tinged lighting transformed the casino into an underwater cavern, with wavy patterns on the walls and columns of golden beams that shone like starlight reaching down toward the ocean floor. When Sloane took a step forward, a school of holographic fish darted out of her path, swirling around the nearest card table before fading away.

A soundtrack of waves and gurgling bubbles played quietly behind the rhythm of jingling slot machines and clattering luck wheels. Cards flipped, men laughed, and serving drones hummed through the space carrying trays of fizzing drinks.

"Not a lux casino," Hilda muttered. "Right."

Vin hadn't mentioned the lux aspect of this casino in his notes. Maybe it hadn't *been* lux, back then. He'd made those notes well before the Bone System's dictator had run off to another galaxy, leaving a lot of relieved people behind.

Maybe the casino had come into its own luck since then. Shard wasn't the kind of place where straight-and-narrow rich people would show their faces, but why shouldn't well-off criminals have a little lux-level fun, too?

While Hilda made her way to the counter to check her knives, Sloane took a good look around the place. She almost felt like she'd gone through a portal to another part of the galaxy. Shard's streets had been defined by torn boots and suspiciously stained sleeves, zigzagging drunks and bulging pockets that hinted of hidden weapons.

Here, the gamblers wore long evening gowns and puffed-out skirts, silk ties, glittering heels. No one was staggering drunk. No one was armed, either, except—she assumed—for the pair of tuxedo-clad guards who watched from either side of the room.

How did the clientele *get* here? Through underground tunnels? A hov-train station, maybe? She glanced up, as if the ceiling could supply the answer, but all it gave her was a holograph of a kraken that devoured a pirate ship as she watched, sending glints of treasure raining down on the casino floor as it feasted.

"All right," Hilda said, returning to Sloane's side. "Where to?"

Sloane looked away from the kraken, trying not to question whether the tableau was meant to be a promise or a threat. Pirates got devoured for stealing, right? No doubt she was overthinking it. "Level C, of course."

Hilda rubbed her nose with the back of her hand. "Didn't the elevator AI say fighting *is* allowed on Level C?"

Sloane grinned. "Yup. Come on."

Three gold-plated escalators later, they emerged in a rooftop garden to the soundtrack of live piano music—and fists pounding into flesh.

Obviously, the casino allowed fighting on Level C. Fighting *was* Level C.

The garden did have plants, enough of them to fill the air with herbal notes, but she couldn't imagine who would come here for a leisurely stroll. Not with the elevated fighting ring that dominated the entire center of the terrace. A gray stone tower surrounded it, recalling some kind of ancient arena. They'd somehow built it so that the ring stood open to the air. Even with a ramp that wrapped around the first floor, the setup made the tower look like it was floating.

On the upper levels, shadows moved inside the walls, people passing beyond the open arched windows or sitting on the edges, shouting and laughing and raising fists as they traded bets around. There were even figures lined around the top edge of the tower—she counted six stories—and she couldn't make out a railing. The casino probably had a force-field or something to keep people from falling into the ring.

Though maybe not. This was the Bone System, after all.

As she watched, a hov-train clanked to a stop far above the tower—they must be well clear of the smog up here—and hovered in midair as a trio of teardrop-shaped cabs broke free from the body of the train. They dropped silently to the top level of the ring, where they discharged their passengers and admitted more before ascending to click back into place.

A beat, and the train took off again, snaking its trackless way through the city like a serpent on the hunt.

That explained how the casino's clientele avoided the streets. Sloane wouldn't have expected to find drop-cabs in a place like Shard, though. Hov-trains were one thing—they were ubiquitous throughout the Parse Galaxy—but drop-cabs added a layer of complication that hinted at infrastructure.

Or innovative thinking. She frowned after the disappearing train, trying to decide if it meant anything. She itched to flick another coin toward the ring, just to see if the grav anchors were tied in with the drop-cab channels.

Even if it didn't tell her anything, it'd make a neat sound when the coin hit the bottom of the pod.

A loud cheer from the crowd jerked her attention away from the sky and back to the matter at hand. She'd have to look into the drop-cabs later. Because there, standing in the center of the ring with his teeth bared and his fists raised, was the bounty whose capture would pay for *Moneymaker*'s repairs.

If she was lucky, and if she was quick, she might be able

to use the tokens to set her own bounty, to find her uncle, and to get back to her real life.

A girl could hope.

Brighton was a huge man, and strong, his upper arms rippling with muscles. And he knew how to use his size to win a fight, if the skyboard was correct; it showed him as winning the last five.

He looked poised to win this one, too. His opponent was half his size and swaying fitfully in the middle of the ring. Sloane was no expert, but the guy seemed half cooked to her.

She managed to take three steps toward the ring before Hilda froze. Not bad, considering. She'd expected the pilot to catch on a beat sooner. "Oh, no," Hilda said. "Dammit to the Fringe, Sloane. You knew Brighton would be here, didn't you?"

Sloane grabbed a flute of sparkling wine from a passing tray and tossed back half the glass, almost choking on the riot of fizzles that crowded down her throat. "Yes," she said. "Yes, I did. See? No robbing. It's a Federation-approved bounty."

"That's what you said last time!"

Yeah, she might've tried to capture Brighton once before.

Sloane rolled the stem of the glass between her fingers. "To be fair, last time *you* found the bounty posting. In *my* ex's things. After *he* betrayed us with his criminal tendencies."

Sloane wasn't sure if he could technically be referred to as her 'ex' if he was dead, but it got the point across.

She *really* hadn't wanted to bring up Oliver.

Hilda crossed her arms again, adding a frown and a

disapproving chin tilt into the mix this time. Clearly not ashamed of her actions, then.

"I just need someone to watch my back," Sloane said. "Can you do that?"

"Do I have a choice?"

"Sure. But the ship only flies when I say it flies, so if I die you'll be stuck on Shard. Not the best place for a summer home, though I've seen worse."

She hadn't, and neither had Hilda. Probably. After a moment of glaring, Hilda grabbed her own flute of wine, gripping the stem so hard Sloane expected it to crack. "I'm going to kill your uncle."

Not if Sloane got to him first.

Trusting Hilda to follow, Sloane made her way to the curving ramp that led into the towering stands, scanning her palm for entry. The passage was dimly lit, castle-like, and it smelled like sweat and old wine. So much for the lux.

Sloane kept half an ear on the ring as she moved toward the top of the tower. She had time; as long as Brighton stayed in the fight, she'd be able to pin him. She ran a finger along the tech inlay in the stone, a thread of black that marbled every inch of the gray walls. This place was well watched.

Every few steps, her foot crossed a gravity anchor pressed into the floor. They weren't nearly as shoddy as the ones on the streets of Shard. Those, she could've displaced with a chisel and a prayer.

Contemplating her options, Sloane emerged onto the top level of the ring, where a burst of wind from a descending drop-cab whipped her hair into a frenzy. As she grabbed for it, Hilda gasped. Still moving, Sloane turned back to see what had scared her.

And ran straight into a midnight-blue Fleet uniform.

Or, more accurately, the chest of the person *inside* the uniform.

Sloane stepped back as the Fleet soldier shot out a hand to steady her, half ready to tell him to get the hell out of here in that uniform before someone stuck a switchblade in his back. But when she looked up at his face, his gray eyes widened in recognition.

It was mirrored, no doubt, in her own expression. Because this man commanded the entire Galactic Fleet. And worse, she'd met him before.

CHAPTER 2

BEHIND HIS SHIELD of blue uniform cloth and gold-plated medals, Commander Fortune had the kind of face that made it impossible to guess his age. There were hints of lines beginning to form at the corners of his eyes, and the tops of his cheeks, but they were neither deep enough to suggest advanced age nor tan enough to imply long hours in the sun. Flecks of gray interrupted his dark hair, which was so richly brown that it bordered on black—making gray hair almost inevitable. Sloane should know; she'd plucked a silver strand out of her own thirty-year-old head last week.

Whatever his age, the Commander was a tall man. Imposing. He was, in fact, looking imposingly down at her now, betraying only a hint of surprise at her presence here. The tick of an eyebrow, nothing more. "Ms. Sinclair, isn't it?" he said.

His voice was both soft and resonant, his fingers gentle as he held onto her elbow. She remembered that voice, and the feeling of wanting to lean in, to hear what he had to say, even when she knew she'd do better to run in the opposite direction.

The last time Sloane had seen Commander Fortune, he'd been staring at her as she'd made her escape from a Fleet ball. After threatening to destroy a priceless sculpture. Among other things.

Her father had managed to shield her from Fleet prosecution—retribution, more like—because he'd believed the whole incident to be nothing more than a witless prank. Even with his intervention, Sloane's reputation in the academy had been destroyed. What'd been left of it, anyway.

The Fleet, though, had been forced to leave her alone. But legal recourse or not, this man clearly hadn't forgotten her.

Fortune knew her real name; he had to. Even had Sloane's father not thrown his weight around on her behalf, that video of her hugging that sculpture had gone viral, her name splashed across the feeds for months. Fortune would have seen it.

She'd made him look like a fool.

Now, she gripped her wineglass, doing her best to steady herself. She couldn't lose her head here. Better to say nothing than to give the game away.

"We've met before," Fortune said, as if she'd responded. As if he was reminding her of something. "Or did you forget?"

She glanced at Hilda, who gave her a *get-it-together* shake of her head. Or maybe it was an *abandon-ship* shake of her head. Sloane couldn't tell. Too late for option B, anyway, and potentially a lost cause for option A.

Hilda blinked, and words traced across Sloane's eye screen. *Skye Sinclair,* the message read. *Your alias at the ball.*

Sloane could've kissed Hilda for the reminder. She

wasn't much for aliases; she had enough to keep track of without a file full of fake names to remember.

She cleared her throat, straightened her back, and looked the Commander straight in the eye. She wasn't sure where this was headed, but she wasn't going to let him taunt her. If that was what he was doing. His expression was impossible to read.

"It's Sloane Tarnish," she said. "Not Sinclair."

He released her elbow, and she startled. She hadn't even realized he'd still been holding it. "I know."

He turned to the nearest arch and looked out at the fight, resting his gloved hands on the ledge. There were fewer people here than there'd been on the way up, which his presence might well explain. These were not the kind of people who wanted to keep company with the Fleet.

"Nice night for a fight," he said. "Are you here for anyone in particular?"

He knows. The words drifted across Sloane's eye screen, another message from Hilda. *He knows we're here for Brighton.*

So what if he did? Brighton might be a Level 14 criminal in the Fleet's books, but the bounty was Federation approved—and that meant the Fleet couldn't stop her from cashing in on it. Even the Fleet captains who'd warned her away from the Bone System in the first place had acknowledged that.

Sure, it had been some kind of a glitch in the system that allowed a Fleet-classed criminal to qualify for a Federation-approved bounty in the first place, and while he'd still been in prison. But Brighton was free now, and ripe for the taking. Whatever that glitch had been, it wasn't her problem.

Sloane narrowly kept from cringing as she realized

Fortune had probably heard about that incident, too. She propped her elbows on the ledge beside him as if leaning in for a better look at the fight, while surreptitiously stretching her fingers toward the far edge. If there was a forcefield protecting the ring, she'd be able to feel it.

"I hear someone released that man from prison," Fortune said, nodding down at the ring.

Yeah, he definitely knew she was here for Brighton. Still gripping her half-empty wine glass in one hand, Sloane pushed the fingers of her other hand past the border of the ledge. No resistance, no sting, no zap. No forcefield.

"I hear it wasn't a Fleet prison at all," Sloane said. "I hear that the Fleet was allowing him to languish on an otherwise abandoned station, where he'd been stashed to rot by a world-crushing dictator."

Fortune's expression changed a bit at that, his lips compressing ever so slightly. It might've been shame, or regret. It was most likely annoyance. "Have you ever tried negotiating with a madman, Ms. Tarnish?"

Only once or twice.

A drop-cab descended to the right, and Sloane tracked its route, hoping she still appeared to be watching Brighton's fight. The droplet-shaped cab hovered *over* the ring when it landed, spilling its passengers into the oversized archways. Interesting.

Sloane sent a silent message to Hilda, who was still hovering near the opposite wall. *Do you know if the hov-trains would be connected to the gravity anchors on a place like this?*

Why do I have a feeling I don't want to answer that?

Sloane could almost hear the pilot's sigh between the words that streamed across her eye screen. But she needed an answer. *Hilda?*

A beat of nothing. Then: *Most cities, the systems would be separate. A place like Shard... I'd say it's fifty-fifty that they rigged them together. Used the grav anchors to counterbalance the trains. Like you said, it would save time and materials.*

And Hilda acted so innocent about the 'trick' Sloane had shown her. Uncle Vin had probably used that one every day. Hilda probably could have harvested a dozen grav anchors from the surface, instead of a measly pair.

Sloane would call her on it later. For now, she needed an exit. *Do the drop-cabs improve those odds?*

Another beat. *Forty-sixty, in favor of dovetailing systems. It's the kind of corner they might cut. Emphasis on the might.*

Magnetic? Like the lift?

I'm not an engineer, but probably. Do I want to know why you're suddenly interested in gravity engineering?

Nope.

Fortune was watching her out of the corner of his eye, as if he knew perfectly well that Sloane wasn't simply watching the fight. Brighton was facing a new partner now —she hadn't seen the fate of the previous one—and by the look of things, he was about to win. Again.

Sloane pinged a last message to Hilda—*Meet me on the ship*—and turned back to the Commander.

"Tell me something, Fortune," she said. "What are you doing in a casino on Shard, of all places?"

He laid his palms out flat on the stone sill, and she imagined he pressing down hard. Holding himself steady. A restrained man. Cautious. "Perhaps I'm securing a Level 14 criminal who escaped from a holding cell. That we had every intention of extracting him from so we could ensure his safety."

Right. Sloane made herself meet the Commander's eyes, though his gaze was unnervingly intense. "But what are *you* doing here? Surely the most powerful man in the galaxy doesn't need to be on the ground for every single Fleet operation."

Was it her imagination, or did he flinch at that? Imagination. It had to be.

"That would be impossible," he said.

"And yet, here you are."

"Perhaps I'm just here to watch the fight."

She couldn't tell if she was getting to him, or if the raw note in his voice was something else. Irritation? Suspicion? It couldn't possibly be amusement.

She really needed to work on reading people better. "You just don't seem like much of a gambler," she said.

He smiled. It was just a quirk of his lips, but it deepened the lines around his eyes. And not in a bad way. "Oh, I'm not."

The crowd reared up, their boos and hisses pinging from every direction, and Sloane whipped her attention back to the center of the ring. Below, a team of Fleet soldiers was surging out of the second level of the tower-ring, leaping from the arched windows in half-covered uniforms. They'd come here in secret. Of course they had.

The soldiers landed, half a dozen of them, each of them bouncing just a tick too high as the floor rippled to absorb the impact. Every last one landed on their feet.

The arches might not have forcefields, but even a Shard casino kept safety mechanisms in the floor. Good to know.

The Fleet soldiers closed in on Brighton to the tune of the angry crowd, elbowing his opponent out of the way so they could clap a pair of magna-cuffs around the big man's wrists. In seconds, they'd secured his hands in front of him while his lips moved frantically, as though he was trying to defend himself with words. Little good that would do.

Above, the hov-train drifted into sight, and Sloane wished she'd started counting the seconds since the drop-cabs had last ascended. The Commander had distracted her.

Never mind. The drop-cabs would be here in a minute, give or take. Sometimes, things lined up so perfectly that it made her want to laugh.

Sloane drained the last of her wine and shoved the glass into the Commander's hand. "Hold this for me, Fortune," she said.

She didn't wait to see if he accepted the glass, or if he let it fall. She swung up onto the ledge and, before she could think too hard about it, she jumped.

The crowd was mercilessly loud as she fell, her hair streaming out behind her so that she wished she'd tied it back. Half the boos and jeers shifted to cheers again as whatever safety force was in the ring floor pushed back against her, vibrating hard enough to make her ribs ache. It felt like a reverse parachute, a field of resistance shoving her up against gravity.

She imagined new bets being passed through the crowd, with her at the center of them, though she had no idea what they would bet on. How long she could stand in the ring without getting shot?

It was better than imagining herself dominating the public feeds, again. Though on a place like Shard, people tended to be more careful about what they photographed.

Sloane's boots hit the floor with a jarring crack, but she kept her footing, managing to push back against the field enough to launch herself back up into a long jump. How did Brighton *fight* down here? It was like taking a stroll through the inside of a bug zapper.

The jump rocketed her past the surprised soldiers, and she threw herself straight into Brighton, knocking him back toward the edge of the ring. The man certainly smelled like he'd been fighting for hours. And eating onions before that.

"What are you doing?" Brighton growled.

She didn't know if he recognized her; she didn't care. Overhead, the drop-cabs began to rain out of the hov-train. She had seconds, now.

A bell jolted over the crowd, a bright, ear-wrenching tone that suggested trouble was on the way. Casino security, more Fleet soldiers, maybe even a good hard zap from the floor.

"You can go with them," she said—shouted, really; she had to, with all the noise, "or you can go with me. Choose."

Brighton took one look at the advancing squad—well-trained soldiers couldn't be put off for long—and his big face blanched. His nose was smashed flat, as though it had been broken so many times it'd just given up. "You. I'll go with you."

Sloane grabbed the man's magnetically cuffed wrists. "Jump." He obeyed, and she jumped with him, wrenching his wrists toward the gravity anchors that dotted the perimeter of the ring. They slammed into the closest one, the magna-cuffs zinging against the gravity anchor with a suction-like charge.

For a second, nothing happened.

Brighton flailed, his arm stretched high above his head, wrists stuck fast to the anchor. "I can't move!"

Above, the drop-cabs discharged their passengers and waited the requisite seconds for new travelers. Sloane couldn't see what was happening on the platform, but she had to guess that no one wanted to leave quite yet.

The squad advanced on them, close enough for one of the soldiers to reach for her leg. If Hilda was wrong, and if Shard hadn't dovetailed their hov-train system with their gravity anchors, Sloane and Brighton would both be in Fleet custody in about half a second.

The drop-cabs started to rise, and Brighton's magnacuffs caught the flow of power between the grav anchor and the drop-cab channel. Sloane grabbed onto his neck as his arms jerked over his head, and he gave a shout of surprise as the magnet whipped them up through the ring.

They moved too fast for her to make out Commander Fortune—assuming he was still watching from the crowd—but she had to imagine she'd surprised him into making another actual expression.

You're a lunatic. Hilda's text was as toneless as the Commander's face was impassive. In Hilda's case, Sloane preferred to imagine the pilot's voice tinged with awe and appreciation. She also preferred to picture herself rising gracefully with the pod, even hooked to Brighton as she was, and would avoid any photograph evidence to the contrary.

The ship, Hilda. Meet us at the next station, would you? I'll key in the codes from here.

On it.

The pod locked onto the hov-train, and Sloane climbed over the still-screaming Brighton to haul herself inside, then bent to help him follow. The hov-train zipped through the city, leaving the casino behind.

CHAPTER 3

GARETH FORTUNE'S soldiers should be laughing at him. They should be angry, and they would be justified in that anger, at the missteps—so *many* missteps—that had led them to lose custody of a Level 14 criminal. Again.

As the shuttle docked and discharged his crew onto the *Sabre*, the soldiers that filed past him merely looked... disappointed. Affronted, perhaps. They'd mounted a perfect ambush, and their target had been swept right out from under them.

"There was nothing we could've done, Commander."

Pitorski was the last soldier out of the shuttle, and Gareth paused when she spoke to him. It might've been his imagination, but he thought the others slowed just a tick on their way into the star frigate. Waiting to see how he'd react. What he'd say.

"She outsmarted us," Pitorski added. "That bounty hunter."

Gareth seriously doubted that Pitorski could be ignorant of Sloane Tarnish's name. The woman's picture had been the talk of the public feeds for weeks after that disaster of a Fleet ball. A viral moment that'd left the galaxy laughing—at Sloane, at the Fleet, and even at the sculptor who had fashioned that monstrosity.

The only wonder there was that Gareth himself had been standing with his back to the cameras, and thus his identity hadn't been confirmed as he'd stared after her with his mouth open like a fish.

It had been guessed at, however.

He shook his head. He should be the one offering encouragement to his soldiers, not accepting it from them. "No, soldier. She got lucky."

Pitorski nodded, but her lips were still twisted like she didn't quite believe it. Fleet soldiers were no fools.

As Pitorski headed off for rest and chow with her squad, Lieutenant Martin Lager met Gareth at the doors to the main corridor, falling into step at his side as he made his way toward the central level of the ship. The *Sabre* was a battle-class star frigate, though Gareth preferred to use her to *stop* battles, rather than engaging in them. After the cramped squalor that defined the atmosphere on Shard, Gareth appreciated her painstakingly polished corridors, and walls that were spaced wide enough to let a quartet pass with room to spare.

Sabre held a crew of three thousand Fleet soldiers, engineers, and scientists, not to mention the arbitrators and diplomatic specialists he insisted on keeping close at hand. She was among the fourteen star frigates that operated under his command, the largest class of ship in the Fleet. He'd flown on *Sabre* for a decade now, and that made her more of a home than anywhere his boots had touched on the ground.

Lieutenant Lager had a fliptab in his hand and a gleam

in his eye that suggested he was ready to launch into a summary of everything that happened during Gareth's short absence. Though not, Gareth suspected, until he'd needled Gareth for information about what'd gone wrong on Shard.

"Updates," Gareth said, hoping to delay whatever questions Lager had on the tip of his tongue.

Lager's pace matched Gareth's as he made his way through the ship, his strides long, his smile wry for some reason. The man laughed more often than not, though, so it could be anything. Lager had brown skin and ears that could prop up his hat without assistance from his skull, if they ever had a chance.

He was a good soldier, and among those Gareth considered his right-hand officers. Which was why Gareth probably *would* tell him exactly what had happened on Shard.

But not right now.

"*Cutlass* and *Katana* are cleaning up the last of the issues between the cartels that'd been battling between Izo and its moon," Lager said. "The cartels agreed to stick to their own territories and allow the Fleet to set up a neutral station in the middle where they can show up to trade. No weapons allowed there, no drugs, no shootouts."

"Good," Gareth said. The Callow Clan and the Mechics had been two of the first organizations to descend on the place, and they had both chosen the planet Izo as their home base. They'd been fighting over the territory ever since.

It was difficult to keep law and order in a system that *had* no laws or order. But the Fleet's job wasn't to stop them from running whatever cons they were running, as long as they stuck to their own territory. The Fleet's job—Gareth's job—was to keep the corruption from spilling into systems that *did* have rules.

Usually, this sort of thing stayed in the outer quadrant of Parse, a problem that was mostly contained in the Fringe Systems. But ever since Adu System's tyrant of a leader had fled to another galaxy, the place had been ripe for chaos as every mid-sized criminal organization in the Parse Galaxy flocked there to stake a claim. Planets, moons, asteroids. They were all overrun.

And Adu—they called it the Bone System, and for good reason—was a Middle System. Not a Fringe. Not an Outer. Smack in the middle of the galaxy and cozied right up to the Fleet's own Cadence System.

"Sure, it's good," Lager agreed. "Until we have to staff our base with people who can't be corrupted."

Gareth clapped him on the shoulder. "Sounds like a Lieutenant-level job. What else?"

"Might be a bit of a skirmish brewing around the Hold. I sent the *Bayonet* to intercede if necessary."

"Good. Keep me updated."

Sloane Tarnish was right about one thing: Gareth didn't need to involve himself directly in ground operations. He didn't even need to command his own ship. Had he wished to, he could make use of the dusty office on Fane, call the shots from a distance. With lieutenants like Lager to update him, it'd be easy enough.

But Gareth had been directly involved in ops since the moment he'd joined up. Sometimes before that. He'd grown up on Fleet ships, and even his father hadn't been able to keep him completely out of the action.

When he'd made Commander, Gareth had continued joining his soldiers on the ground. At first, it'd been to prove himself, and to prove to them that he hadn't just landed this job because his father held the position before him. In the process, though, he'd learned that it was important not to forget the feeling of action on the ground.

It forced him to stay sharp. More importantly, it forced him to remember what he risked every time he sent soldiers on a mission.

Lager coughed. "So," he said, "outsmarted you again, did she?"

Slick subject change. Leave it to Lager. Gareth didn't slow his pace. "How did you manage to get through your reports before bringing that up?"

Lager shrugged. "Wing and a prayer, sir."

Trust the man to be amused by the situation. Gareth squeezed his hands into fists, then released them. Good stress relief, that. He was still wearing his gloves, and he removed them now, tucking them into the pocket of his uniform jacket. "It doesn't count as *outsmarting* when your opponent disregards the rules."

And the laws of physics. How had the woman known the ring's grav anchors would be connected with the hov-train channels? That wasn't standard, at all.

Had she known? Or had it been the wildest lucky guess in history? She seemed prone to those. Either way, what in the vacuum's name had given her idea to *use* them like that?

He hoped she hadn't seen his face as she'd used his own soldiers' magna-cuffs to ride the hov-channel from the ring to the drop-cab. Of all the ridiculous, idiotic, madcap ideas he'd ever heard of.

"Brighton *is* listed as a Federation bounty again," Lager said. "I checked."

Of course he was. Gareth clenched his jaw, and his molars creaked. He was going to grind them into dust, if he wasn't careful. "They're overreaching. Again. Call the

Commission into an emergency meeting. We need to address this."

Lager snorted. "They're not going to like that."

No, they would not. Too bad. "I want them in the V-Space by the time I've changed my boots."

He could use a filter to hide Shard's dust from his clothing, but he preferred not to face the Fleet Advisory Commission with an asterisk over his profile. They might think he was hiding something more dangerous than dirty boots.

Gareth hated politics. But the Fleet's peacekeeping operation depended on both financial and diplomatic support from the systems—at least the Center and Middle Systems—so politics were part of the job.

"Half of Halorin System's asleep right now," Lager said. "We can't rouse every world leader in the galaxy just because the Federation's misbehaving again. If you'll wait for—"

"I appreciate the warning, Lieutenant," Gareth interrupted. "Wake them up."

Lager shook his head, then popped a salute. "On it, sir. V-Space in five." He took off down the corridor at a half-run, his boots clicking on the polished floor.

Gareth suppressed a sigh. He wasn't in any state to speak to the Commission, but he didn't see what choice he had. If they didn't deal with the Cosmic Trade Federation's continued interference in Fleet affairs, they'd face much worse headaches later on.

Best to make sure the Commission fully understood the seriousness of the matter, so they could take action.

Besides, Gareth didn't call emergency sessions very often. Once a year, perhaps. Twice at most. Today might be the third, but this year had been a special case.

Gareth didn't drag his feet in changing his boots and washing his face—he needed a shave and wasn't sure when he'd get it—but he didn't rush, either. When it came to the Commission, he had precious few tools at his disposal, and the ability to keep them waiting was one of them.

He wondered if it would surprise Sloane Tarnish to learn how often he had to leverage clean boots and late arrivals. The most powerful man in the galaxy, indeed. He'd have expected her to know better; her father was a Center-System dignitary.

The V-Space was full by the time he entered the meeting, joining the call directly from his cabin. The round-table design expanded as each newcomer arrived, but Gareth's eye screen didn't alert him to any missing members when he entered. An emergency meeting brought everyone to the table, whether they'd been asleep or not.

The Commission could have arranged the V-Space in any way they liked. A stadium. A classroom. A meadow. But the setup had been the same for as long as Gareth had commanded the Fleet, and well before that.

He didn't know who'd chosen the round-table design, with dozens of seats; it never would have worked in a physical meeting room. But the V-Space allowed cameras to zoom, conversations to shift, and perspectives to change. It would be dizzying, he supposed, to someone who hadn't been visiting the space off and on since he'd taken his first steps. Perhaps before that, even.

Gareth had to admit that a round table negated any trouble when it came to hierarchies or jostling for power. The problem was that the Fleet Commander had to stand in the center to make his reports. It always made him feel... Well, the way the fighters must feel when they fought in that tower-ringed stage on Shard. Watched, attacked, and undoubtedly the subject of a wager or two.

Rarely did the Commission members all agree on anything, yet today might prove the exception as every last face looked at him with furrowed brows, pursed lips, or narrowed eyes. Not happy to be awoken from their silk-lined beds. Not happy at all.

Good thing Lager wasn't here to say, 'I told you so.'

It was Alisa March who spoke first. A thin, matronly woman with red hair, she represented a trio of planets in the Torrent System. He'd long considered her an ally and a friend, though today she looked just as irritated as everyone else.

"All right, Commander," Alisa said, "you have our attention. Some of us dragged ourselves out of bed to be here. What's your emergency?"

They could still be *sitting* in bed, in some cases, but it was probably best not to point that out.

"The Cosmic Trade Federation is interfering with the Fleet's business yet again," he said. "They—"

"—interrupted an operation of yours rather dramatically, I'd say."

That was Osmond Clay. A blanched raisin of a man, his hair transparently blond, his eyes like watery blue filters. He wore gray robes with golden fringe along the sleeves. Gareth had never seen him wear anything else.

Clay spoke with half a laugh in his voice. Amused. Content, even, as if he'd been waiting for this call. Looking forward to it, perhaps.

Clay *wasn't* an ally, and he certainly wasn't a friend. He led a System that would have been too small to be of any consequence, had it not been the lead manufacturer of data chips in the galaxy. "We've all seen what happened by now, Fortune."

Clay might know about the incident on Shard, but many of the other reps were no doubt scanning the feeds for information. It hadn't even been an hour yet, and most of them had been sleeping. Clay took the opportunity to lean back in his chair and prop his hands behind his head. He, at least, seemed happy to be here.

Any chance to humiliate Gareth always seemed well worth Clay's while. Why that was the case, Gareth didn't know, but the man always took every opportunity to undermine him, interrupt him, and try to make him look like a fool.

The operative word being *try*.

"What do you care if the Federation sends some lowlife bounty hunter after a target?" Clay asked. "Makes your job easier, eh Fortune?"

Sloane Tarnish was a lot of things, but *lowlife* wasn't one of them. A sapphire in a mud heap, more like. The thought landed in his brain without warning or context, and he very nearly grimaced. He ought to be comparing the woman to a snake, or a scavenger. Maybe a mole, popping up from the depths to steal what was his—but damn him if the sapphire didn't stick in his mind like she'd slipped it there intentionally. Perhaps she had.

Shaking Sloane out of his brain, Gareth opened his mouth to respond, but Clay held up a hand. "Perhaps you've got too much on your plate as it is, trying to get Adu System under control."

The implication being that the Bone System *wasn't* in control, and that Gareth was responsible for that. Rather than whatever had drawn the System's blight of a dictator out of the galaxy, leaving a power vacuum to suck up every criminal mind in the galaxy. The place was primed to explode.

What *had* Sloane been doing on Shard? There were plentiful bounties available throughout the galaxy, most of them in much more pleasant systems. Why Brighton? Why Shard?

Clay opened his mouth again, but enough was enough. Was Gareth the Commander of the Fleet, or a carpet to be walked on? "The Fleet protected Cappel from Fringe incursion just last year, Clay. We lost half a dozen star corvettes and a platoon of cubes, all of them full of good soldiers."

Before Clay could respond, Gareth pointed to Seamus Wen, the president of a Middle System planet called Korvish. He sat beside Clay, his back ramrod straight, his attention fixed on Gareth. "We prevented asteroid annihilation in Korvish before that," Gareth said. "And arbitrated a ceasefire in Torrent System, Alisa, before *that*."

Alisa wouldn't be here if the Fleet hadn't made that truce happen; Torrent's inner planets would have obliterated her little union of worlds.

"No one's questioning the necessity of the Fleet." Alisa's tone was placating, though Clay's smirk said *he* might be questioning it. He wouldn't be smiling like that if the Fleet had allowed that Fringe cartel to overrun his factories last year. "We all rely on your support."

On his battleships, more like. But only when it was convenient for them. Gareth made himself relax his hands. He prided himself on staying cool. He *had* to. But stars, how he hated politics. "We're meant to be curbing violence," he said. "I'm afraid the Federation is infringing on our jurisdiction because they want a big payday from the cartels. They could be delivering bounties back to their people, for freedom or for punishment."

The cartels might want to rescue their people from prosecution, though in many cases Gareth suspected they wanted to enact their own brand of justice.

"The point of the Federation is to prevent that, Commander," Alisa said. "Every bounty gets delivered to the CTF for processing before the person is released to the requestor. You know the rules."

Yes, he knew the rules. They were, by and large, rules that put the Federation in a position of unmatched power, at least for those without star frigates at their disposal. It was the Fleet's job, and Gareth's responsibility, to protect them *all*. Criminals, innocents, and everyone in between.

"I want a meeting with the Federation," Gareth said. "Surely someone here can arrange that."

Frowns deepened. Fingers rubbed chins. Knuckles tapped on knees, and toes tapped uncomfortably, but no one answered. Not one. He was speaking to a virtual room full of the most powerful people in the galaxy, and none of them wanted to arrange a meeting with the organization that supposedly helped facilitate trade for all of them. Could no one see a problem with that?

Osmond Clay sat up in his chair, steepling his fingers together at his chest. Trust the man to take advantage of any chance to fill a silence. "We all understand the little Galactic Fleet versus Cosmic Trade Federation rivalry." He kept that same smirk on his lips, like he was issuing a gentle lecture to a tantrum-throwing five-year-old. "But let's stay on task, shall we?"

Never mind. A five-year-old would find that condescending, too.

Gareth waited for someone else to speak, but no one did. When he glanced at Alisa, she simply gave her head a minuscule shake. She couldn't help him on this.

"Move to adjourn," Clay said.

Gareth didn't see who seconded. It didn't matter. He was suddenly achingly tired, and hungry, too. He shouldn't have bothered. Half of these people were probably in the Federation's pocket, or deeply invested at the very least. Perhaps even with their own planetary funds. They had to protect their interests.

One by one, the galaxy's world leaders blinked out of sight, until Gareth stood alone in the V-Space with Osmond Clay. Who, for some reason, hadn't scurried back to his money machine on Cappel.

"What can I do for you, Clay?" Gareth was almost proud that he'd managed to eke the words out without adding an expletive.

"Just needed a private word, Commander."

"Then have it."

Clay chuckled. "Oh, no. I need to have it on Cappel. It's not the kind of conversation one has in a V-Space. You understand." Gareth didn't, but it wasn't a question, and Clay didn't stop talking long enough for him to protest. "You don't mind, do you? We're just a hop and a skip from Adu System. You *are* still in Adu, yes?"

Gareth was grinding his teeth again, and he made himself stop. Right now, he didn't care how powerful Osmond Clay was, or how many data chips his factories rained into the galaxy every year—or even how badly the Fleet needed those chips to function.

Right now, he needed to show his teeth.

"I'll add you to the list," Gareth said. "Maybe you can handle whatever little *rivalry* you're dealing with on your own."

"You—"

It was satisfying, far too satisfying, to watch Clay's

expression melt from smug satisfaction to open-mouthed surprise as Gareth ended the meeting. He'd pay for that later, no doubt, but it would be worth it.

The most powerful man in the galaxy, indeed. If only Sloane Tarnish could see him now.

CHAPTER 4

SLOANE FELT FAIRLY confident about the last-minute brig she'd set up for Brighton. Whatever her uncle had been hauling—or pretending to haul—before he disappeared, he'd hauled it in huge plasterboard crates. And once she'd rigged the stolen set of Fleet magna-cuffs to make a lock, the crate made an excellent cell. She didn't think even Brighton could break the slats, though so far the big man had just been sitting there, picking his nails and throwing out occasional comments.

The only problem was that the crates were too heavy to move, and the one where Brighton now rested his laurels was right next to a cluster of *Moneymaker*'s system controls. Everything that wasn't stuffed into engineering—a room that Sloane had so far managed to avoid, mostly—was right here in cargo.

Which meant that Brighton had been heckling her for the last hour while she watched the ship's science officer trying to install the new onboard AI. Sloane had picked up the unit on her way out of Shard, much to Hilda's consternation.

"Thought she'd be done by now," Brighton said as Alex connected a bunch of rainbow-colored wires and inserted data chips into data-chip holders. Sloane didn't know their official names. "It's not all that complicated."

Brighton's voice was as thick as his neck, but he sounded more bored than anything else. He had no reason to complain. Sloane had given him water, and a snack. She'd gotten him away from the Fleet. What more could the man want? Aside from the obvious don't-turn-me-in-to-the-Federation request.

"I'm not a computer scientist." Alex's head was half-buried in the box of wires, her red hair tied on up top of her head in a thick bun. "I'm an astrophysicist."

"An out-of-work one," Sloane said. Alex had studied wormholes, dedicated her life to them, and even created one —before discovering that *using* wormholes could potentially implode the universe, and that she'd better stop playing with them. Now, she seemed to be at loose ends, unsure of what to do next.

Sloane figured the task would be good for her. Get her out of her room, which was starting to smell like the cheesy snacks Alex liked. Get her working on a new problem.

"I thought you were going to hire a security officer," Hilda said. The pilot had set *Moneymaker* on auto while they orbited a random asteroid near Shard. Most likely another sliver of destroyed planet, but Sloane tried not to think too much about that. Hilda was smoking one of the flowery-smelling rolls that she usually saved for the quiet hours of the night.

Sloane couldn't blame her for being on edge after the show on Shard. She still had adrenaline bursting through her own veins after that, to be honest.

"We can't afford a double-cross-proof security officer,"

Sloane said, "because I can't get through to the Federation to ask them to front us the tokens."

Sloane held up her fliptab, which had been repeatedly dialing the Federation offices for the last fifteen million years, give or take. She had their auto message memorized. *Thanks for your call! Please refer to your bounty posting for delivery instructions. Have a great day!*

"They won't front you the tokens," Brighton said.

Hilda squinted at Alex's work, though Sloane doubted she knew any more about installing ship AIs than Sloane did. "But we can afford a state-of-the-art ship AI."

"Oh, no," Sloane said, "we definitely can't. This is a discount model."

She'd picked it up at Shard's spaceport, in the kind of hole-in-the-wall shop that would switch locations every day, if it'd happened to be located in a place that cared about enforcing laws and things like that.

"I think it's used," Alex said, her voice muffled by cords.

Brighton snorted. "That means stolen."

"Wonderful." Hilda let out a puff of perfume-laced smoke. It smelled distinctly judgmental.

A click sounded from Sloane's fliptab, and the figure of an annoyed-looking Federation official popped into view, his hands on his hips, a knit cap tugged down over his skull. Everyone looked diminutive when you shrank them down into holographic fliptab figures, but this one looked particularly flick-able. Like an angry little elf. "You're tying up the line," he said.

There was no way the Cosmic Trade Federation had one comm line in and out of their facility. "I am not," she said.

The angry little scowl deepened, along with Sloane's urge to flick him. "No, you're not," he said. "But your number's come through approximately ninety-two times in the last hour."

"That doesn't sound approximate."

"Stop calling. Have a great day."

He really didn't look as if he meant it.

"Wait," Sloane said, flashing her fliptab up and over her shoulder so he could get a look at Brighton, whose wide face should be more than recognizable between the slats of the crate. "We picked up Brighton. But I can't get him to you without—"

"Ms. Tarnish, we don't take calls, and we don't negotiate. We accept bounty deliveries at Bay 35 of our headquarters in the Pike System, as every single bounty posting clearly states."

"Told you," Brighton said. He didn't have to sound so pleased, though she supposed she couldn't blame him under the circumstances.

Sloane straightened her back and lifted her chin, narrowly deciding against the addition of a hair flip. It wouldn't look right in holograph. "Then I would like to speak with a manager."

The mini Federation official rolled his eyes, then flickered out of sight as he ended the call.

Sloane started to dial again, but a voice cut her off. It seemed to come from everywhere at once—the floor, the ceiling, even the walls of Brighton's crate—but that had to be an illusion. Something about acoustics.

"Welcome to the ship," the voice said, its tone almost as cheerful as the recorded Federation message but much less squeaky. "I am BRO, your onboard AI. During this fifteen-minute tour, I will orient you to the features of the *Grendel*."

Sloane cringed. Not stolen. Not stolen at all. "*Money-maker*," she corrected.

"Confirmed. I will orient you to the features of the *Moneymaker*."

"Did it just welcome us to our own ship?" Hilda asked.

Sloane decided to find it charming.

"Please accompany me on a tour of the facilities," BRO said.

Alex sat back on her heels and brushed her hands together, though Sloane seriously doubted it was very dirty in those boxes. "What does BRO stand for?"

"Why do we think it stands for anything?" Sloane asked. "Maybe it's got a sister."

"I am the Best Robotic Operative," BRO said.

Okay, so it stood for something. Alex squinted at the box of cords. "You're not robotic."

A pause. "I'm not?"

Sloane stood, folding her fliptab with a click. She was never going to hear the end of this one.

"You're not an operative either," Hilda said.

"I'm *not*?"

"And I seriously doubt he's the best," Brighton put in.

BRO sniffed. "Hurtful."

Sloane held up a hand. "Let's try not to traumatize the AI. BRO, you're the one who's new to the ship. I'm Sloane. Alex is the one who installed you. Hilda's the pilot."

"And the man in the box is Brighton Walsh." BRO actually sounded proud, as if it'd passed a test of some kind. "He's a Level 14 criminal, according to the Fleet database."

Sloane grimaced. "I hope that was a public database."

"Nope!" BRO said cheerfully.

Excellent. "K, no hacking the Fleet," Sloane said. "For the moment, anyway."

Hilda somehow managed to simultaneously raise her eyebrows and glare at Sloane, her cigarette half-raised to her mouth.

"What?" Sloane said. "We might need to hack the Fleet someday. You don't know."

"I think we've crossed them enough," Hilda said, "don't you?"

It was satisfying to beat them, in Sloane's opinion. They were worthy opponents. But sadly, Hilda was right; Sloane really didn't need another run-in with them, or their stone-faced Commander.

Sloane's fliptab chimed, and she opened it to find a new holographic figure staring at her, looking as surprised to see her as she was to see him. This one had a wiry frame, with hard muscles sharpening his arms and shoulders, which were visible, because he wore a vest over bared arms. Tattoos flickered up and down his skin, though she couldn't tell if they were really moving or if it was a trick of the holo.

He had a razor in one hand, and his face was half covered in a layer of white shaving cream.

Alex sighed. "Why do I have a bad feeling about this?"

"I have connected you with the Cosmic Trade Federation manager," BRO said. "They do not *have* a manger, actually, but this man's title is listed as a synonym for the term in the seventy-four thesauruses I checked."

"See?" Sloane said. "Good AI."

"You're going to have to let me know how you did that," the holographic man said. "And I'm a... coordinator."

He didn't look much like a coordinator. He looked like the guy who showed up at your door in the middle of the night to collect on a debt owed. A not-unattractive guy who showed up at your door, but, nevertheless.

"Hey," Sloane said. "Sorry about the AI. It's new."

"I'm a good AI," BRO said.

The 'coordinator' bent, his head disappearing for a second. When he returned, the shaving cream was gone. He was still holding onto the razor, though. "What is it, Ms. Tarnish? Yes, yes, I know who you are. Don't look so surprised. I'd have known even if you hadn't gone viral when you crashed that Fleet party last year. Your father, hm?"

Yes, her father. Household name dignitary nonsense. He was everywhere, even when she hadn't seen him in a year. Great. "I don't want to take too much of your time, Mr.?"

She paused, waiting for him to supply a name, but he just said, "Then don't."

Right. Straight to business. "We need an advance on Brighton's bounty. You can see that we have him, right here, but my ship won't make it all the way to the Pike System. It can't travel the Currents right now, and—"

"Do you know how many things can go wrong in transit?" the coordinator-slash-thug asked. "Bandits. Misfortunes. The bounty's cohorts showing up to spring him. If we paid out on every bounty before we had the man in hand, we'd lose half of them to double-crossing alone. Why collect on a man once when you can collect on him twice, hm?"

"But I won't—"

"I believe my assistant reminded you of the policy, Ms. Tarnish. You want to play bounty hunter, you play by our rules. You take the job, you get the bounty all the way to us. Then we pay."

"Plus expenses?"

"No."

The nameless Federation coordinator blinked out of sight.

"Rude," BRO said.

Sloane closed the fliptab again and shoved it into her pocket, trying to hide her disappointment as she sat down hard on the floor of the cargo hold. It was bad enough to take a call like that on your own, but Hilda and Alex already thought she was a screwup, and Brighton was supposed to be a prisoner. Under her thumb and awed by her power. Or something.

She needed a minute to think, and she couldn't do it when Alex was staring at her with plaintively blue eyes, or while Hilda tapped her fingers on her knees like an angry grandma.

"Right," Sloane said. "No problem. Surely there are other places in the System to secure a bounty gig."

"What good is it if they won't pay until you get there?" Hilda said. "You could shove fifty bounties in crates down here. You have no way to get them to the Federation."

Sloane tapped her fingertips on her knees, thinking. Federation rules meant that bounties could only be delivered to legitimate parties—through the Federation itself, as the coordinator and his flunky had so condescendingly reiterated—but there had to be plenty of people who wanted to find someone off the CTF's books.

There weren't many rules that applied to the entire galaxy, but when the Federation and the Fleet agreed on something, it basically amounted to a universal law. There was illegal, and then there was *illegal*, and bounty rules were strictly enforced.

Sloane licked her lips. "Not a Federation-approved bounty. An independent bounty."

Hilda shook her head, and Alex went white. Even Brighton dropped his face into his hands.

But Brighton, he was the key. Sloane twisted to look at him. "Where would I find a posting like that?"

He rubbed his face, then dropped his hands. "They don't just fall from the sky, girl. You get in contact with a criminal org. If they trust you, they might give you the job."

"Lucky for us, the Bone System's crawling with criminals. Any ideas where we should try?"

"Even if I had one, I wouldn't tell you."

"Why, because I'm going to turn you in, too?"

"No, because they'll cut you up and serve you for dinner."

She'd like to see them try it. Before she could say as much, the ship shuddered, sending her stumbling into Brighton's crate. Alex caught hold of the railing to steady herself.

Before the shuddering had stopped, Hilda was leaping to her feet, heading for the spiral staircase that led up toward the flight deck.

Sloane righted herself more slowly. "BRO? What's happening?"

"We're under attack!" The AI sounded so cheerful; it might have been wishing her a happy birthday. "Did you know your shields are not functioning at optimal capacity?"

Yeah, she knew. She wheeled around to look at Brighton, the Federation coordinator's warning ringing in her ears. Her prisoner's face was flushed, his lips trembling. "Your people?" she asked.

"I don't *have* people." Brighton wedged his bottom lip between his teeth. It made him look like he was eating a caterpillar. "What do the ships look like?"

"They're beautiful!" BRO answered. Gushed. There had to be a way to dial back the thing's... enthusiasm. "They have wings tucked into their sides, but they're not using them right now. They must look like butterflies when they fly in a planet's atmosphere!"

Moneymaker shuddered again, and Brighton sat down hard, tucking himself into the far corner of the crate like a crab retreating into its shell. Not an easy feat, for such a huge man. And it wouldn't do him any good if the ship exploded.

"That would be Fox Clan," Brighton said. "I might've hacked their systems. They'd like to kill me, if possible."

Great. That was just great. Suppressing a curse, Sloane bounded up the steps to join Hilda on the flight deck.

CHAPTER 5

SLOANE'S PRESENCE on the flight deck wasn't strictly necessary, at the best of times. In fact, she got the distinct impression that Hilda preferred her absence. Uncle Vin might've been *Moneymaker*'s captain, but Sloane was more like its... Steward.

Still, she found it was best not to hide out when they were under attack, so she flopped into the co-pilot's seat beside Hilda and strapped in, squinting out the viewport to get a look at their new enemies. She hated to admit it, but BRO was right—the ships were beautiful. Elegant, even, with delicately curved noses and wings tucked into the sides of their bodies, like the translucent beauties you might see on a dragonfly.

She wouldn't have expected a criminal org to put such an emphasis on aesthetics. Pretty or not, though, the ships looked too small to be responsible for *Moneymaker*'s insistent shaking. As she watched, a plasma round blasted out of the closest ship to shower *Moneymaker*'s protective force-field, sending the shield-integrity needles diving toward zero.

"How are those ships hurting our shields?" she asked.

"Our shields suck, for starters," Hilda said.

"I said that!" BRO sounded far too pleased to have gotten something right.

If Sloane were piloting the enemy ship, she'd have saved the plasma blast for after she'd taken the shields out. On a ship with fully-functioning shields, those hits would result in negligible damage. Either these Fox Clan thugs knew *Moneymaker* was in tough shape, or they didn't have anything more serious to blast at the ship.

A year ago, she'd been trying to decide between a career in Nano Healing or Gene Therapy. And now here she was, analyzing the battle tactics of a criminal cartel. It was more than a bit alarming.

But it was what it was. Sloane leaned over the dash and opened comms, choosing the widest channel she could.

"What are you doing?" Hilda asked. "Stop touching my things."

Sloane ignored her. "Hey, Fox Clan. Stop shooting at us, and we might be open to making a deal."

Hilda's braid thumped against the back of her chair—she'd flung it over to keep it out of the way—as she shook her head. "No dice, Sloane. They'll kill him."

Sloane muted the comm. "Just find us a place to land."

"On a random Adu asteroid?"

"Find a moon. Whatever."

"What moon? There's no *planet*!"

"Just do it."

Hilda cursed under her breath—at least, Sloane thought she cursed; she said the words in some language Sloane didn't recognize—but she tilted the ship away from the asteroid and raced away from it at top speed. Or rather, at the top speed that *Moneymaker* was probably capable of at the moment. The squealing sound that ground out from somewhere under her feet suggested that the pilot might be pushing a little too far, but Sloane wasn't about to complain.

Sloane's stomach flipped as Hilda dipped them around another pocket of space rocks. She switched the comm back on. "Hello?"

There was a beat of static, during which the plasma rounds seemed to slow. Though that might have been her imagination. "Hand over the hacker," a raspy voice said. He even sounded villainous. Did they take classes on how to make their voices threatening?

Sloane leaned over the dash. At least he was talking to her. That was something. "How much are you offering?"

"Your life, and you'll be lucky to have that much. Prepare to be boarded."

"Sloane," Hilda hissed, but Sloane held up a hand. Hilda might not think Sloane was in charge here, but she was, and that meant handling bad guys when they surfaced. Which happened a lot more often than she'd have guessed before she'd set out to find her uncle.

"My life's not worth as much as the Federation's reward for this bounty," Sloane said. "Final offer?"

In answer, the Fox Clan ships blasted out a triple burst of plasma, like a coordinated spitting match. *Moneymaker*'s shields stuttered, and Hilda hit a button that sent laser fire plummeting out of the ship's turrets. It burst against the Fox Clan's intact shields like fireworks.

"We're low on ammo," Hilda said.

"We're low on everything." Sloane stabbed the nav screen on the dashboard, hoping Hilda was too busy to slap her hands away. "Here. Olton Moon."

"What's it a moon *of*?"

"Whatever planet used to be made of these asteroids." The Bone System was nothing if not consistent. How long ago the planet had been destroyed, she didn't know; long enough for a city to infest Shard's surface. A couple decades, maybe? The rest of the galaxy had been sidestepping this system for more than a century, and its history was well shrouded.

For good reason, clearly.

Hilda dodged around rocks, using them as a barrier against the plasma. Sloane didn't know where those sleek little ships hid so much ammo, but Hilda was smart to run out the clock. Get them to keep shooting.

Pebbles spattered against the shields, the viewport clouded with dust as *Moneymaker* spun its way toward the moon that the nav screen claimed still existed. She wasn't sure what they'd do if it didn't, only that tossing Brighton out of a window wasn't an option.

"What's your plan after landing on this moon?" Hilda asked.

Sloane licked her lips. "Hide."

"That," BRO said, "is a terrible plan!"

"It's not terrible, it's just underdeveloped. There." Sloane pointed out of the viewport, though Hilda's eyes were locked on the dash screens. "Drop into atmo there."

Hilda pulled the ship toward the Olton Moon—former moon, Sloane supposed; she didn't know what the sphere of rock would be called now, officially—and she studied the surface. Or she attempted to; clouds of mist roiled up from the ground, obscuring the view.

She didn't know much about surface dynamics or atmosphere management. Still, she would have expected whatever had blasted Olton Moon's planet apart to strip its atmosphere. But it either hadn't done that, or the atmosphere had had time to be redeveloped. With intervention, she assumed.

The mist was thick, but the instruments detected breathable air. What was hiding down there?

Undeterred by *Moneymaker*'s approach on Olton, the Fox Clan ships followed her into the atmosphere. Two of them flanked *Moneymaker*, unfurling their wings as the air thickened. They really *were* pretty ships.

"Drop lower. We can lose them in the mist," Sloane said.

"Objection," BRO said. "My data informs me that Olton Moon's surface features an average temperature well below freezing. As I've just found new life on *Moneymaker*, I would object to freezing to death now."

"Nav says there's a settlement there," Sloane said. "How bad can it be?"

Hilda punched a sequence of buttons on the dash, and *Moneymaker* started to descend. She might not like Sloane's idea, but at least she was willing to go with it. "Nav says there are *buildings* there. Not the same as a settlement."

"I do not know who Nav is," BRO replied, "but his data doesn't sound complete."

"The navigation system," Sloane said, "and it isn't."

To the right, the dragonfly-winged ship spun its plasma guns so that Sloane was looking right down the barrel.

The ship to the left did the same.

"Hilda," she said. "Drop."

Moneymaker dropped, but not quickly enough. The blasts shook the hull from both sides, sending alarm sirens ringing throughout the ship. The shield needles dropped below zero, and Sloane thought she heard BRO sob. That thing definitely needed to be recalibrated. If they survived this.

"One more hit, and they'll have us," Hilda said. "There's nothing I can do. We're limping too hard."

The Fox Clan guns were primed, their ships ready to shoot. Sloane shut her eyes.

Nothing happened.

The ship dropped again to the tune of Hilda's stream of curses, leaving Sloane's stomach behind. She swallowed hard, hating space travel more than ever, then opened her eyes.

The Fox Clan ships were gone. In their place were a dozen Fleet-class cube ships, the kind that could break away from a larger vessel and fly independently or re-form into new shapes. At least, that was what Uncle Vin's information said.

She was going to be really annoyed if the Commander had just saved her ass.

"The Fleet doesn't have boots on the ground in the Bone System," Hilda said.

Sloane snorted. "Clearly, we don't know all." She tapped the comm system. "Thanks for the assist, guys. Any chance you've got a base down there? Our ship's in bad shape."

The response came so quickly that it had to be from an onboard android or AI. "You are not authorized to land." The voice was deep-toned, smooth and sure. "Turn back."

"On the Fleet's order?" Sloane asked.

"Abort your attempt to land, or we will be forced to open fire."

"Why bother letting us live this long?" Hilda muttered.

The question sounded rhetorical, but the smooth voice responded. "Those ships had criminal idents. They opened fire on a civilian vessel, and we retaliated. Now abort your attempt to land, or we will be forced to open fire."

"Good enough for me." Hilda flipped a switch, and *Moneymaker* headed back up into the black, rattling hard as it left Olton Moon to shrink into the distance behind them. The Fleet ships maintained their formation just above the cloud cover, watching. Sloane had no doubt they'd intercept any attempt to land.

She sat back in her seat, surprised to note that her hands were shaking. She dragged her fingers through her hair, forced a shaky breath into her lungs. Space battles made her feel helpless. It was hard to pull a trick with magnets when you had cannons on your tail. Impossible to pull a con.

"Well!" BRO said, interrupting the silence. "That was lucky!"

Lucky, and strange. She opened her fliptab, as much for something to do as anything else, and started searching. Hilda was right; the Fleet didn't have any bases in the Bone System.

At least, none that they advertised. They pretended to be so transparent, so upright with their intentions, but Uncle Vin had believed the Fleet had nefarious plans for the galaxy. He'd been sure that they wanted to take it over and rule as a central authority, and he wasn't the only one.

His suspicions, though, might've been the reason he'd disappeared. Had he found a hidden Fleet base, like the one on Olton Moon? Had he tried to interfere?

"What do we do now?" Hilda said. "*Moneymaker*'s even more damaged than it was before. We have no shields and almost no ammo."

"We're also running at forty-seven percent speed capacity!" BRO added cheerfully.

Sloane had a feeling that was the least of the damage. At this point, the poor ship had more broken parts than working ones. They had no onboard mechanic, and her own knowledge was desperately poor. She was OK with tech, if not great, but if it didn't involve Nano Healing, then she was mostly floundering in the dark. They needed to get to a place with a reputable service station, one that could run a full diagnostic and complete a full repair.

How in the galaxy they were going to afford that... But it was the same old problem, the same issue they'd been dealing with since Uncle Vin had disappeared, ditching his ship and his crew, and leaving Sloane to deal with them. Every time she took a step forward, the galaxy threw her three steps back.

Maybe she was going to have to take a dish-washing gig, after all.

"Good news!" BRO said. "I have located an illegal bounty posting in the vicinity!"

Sloane exchanged a glance with Hilda, whose eyebrows ticked so high they nearly brushed her gray hairline. "You found... How?"

"I hacked the Fox Clan's database while they attacked us, as Brighton suggested! I gained access before they exploded."

Sloane had a feeling that was not the kind of criminal-organization contact Brighton had meant. Though hadn't he said he was in trouble with Fox Clan for hacking their networks? Maybe that *was* what he'd meant.

"Okay," Sloane said. "That's... not great."

"Oopsie," BRO said. The AI sounded the way a dog looked after chewing its owner's best slippers.

Hilda, though, looked thoughtful. "Actually," she said, "it might work."

Sloane opened her mouth, then closed it. Hilda shrugged. "We *are* still going after Vin. Right?"

Sloane wanted to ask how it could even be a question,

but Uncle Vin had disappeared months ago, and it felt like she'd been spinning her wheels ever since. Trying to get money so she could traipse around the galaxy in search of him, when she had none of his contacts, none of his underworld know-how. She had no money to pay for information or set a bounty—and was constantly getting sucked into one disastrous situation after another. They'd been to another *galaxy* and back, and they were no further along than they'd been at the start.

"Of course we are," Sloane said.

Hilda swiveled her seat to face Sloane, palms pressed into her knees. If she was shaken from the battle, she didn't show it. "No more side quests, no more galivanting. We get the tokens to fix the ship so we can reach the Federation. Then we turn Brighton in so we can get more money, and we use to find Vincent."

"That's the plan."

Hilda nodded, businesslike. "Then we take whatever bounty BRO found for us. We get the tokens. And we move forward. You *are* ready to move forward?"

Sometimes it felt like there were a hundred reasons not to. But the thought that popped into her mind right now was one that hadn't occurred to her, that she hadn't even known she was afraid to face. Maybe not until those Fleet ships had popped up out of Olton Moon's mist, reminding her that her uncle had stepped into a political minefield when he'd had her lift Fleet intelligence out from under the Commander's nose last year. And that his theories about the Fleet's intentions might be very, very dangerous.

On a subconscious level, it must have occurred to her. But she'd never let herself think the words. Now that they'd formed, though, they stuck in her mind like a bad dream: what if Uncle Vin was dead?

But she couldn't say that. Hilda was relying on her, and so was Alex. Even BRO was relying on her, now. Throat dry, she nodded, trying to look as certain as she knew she ought to feel. "Yes. Ready."

Hilda turned back to the dash. "Set the coordinates, BRO. Let's chase down an illegal bounty."

CHAPTER 6

DESIGNED to house soldiers for months and sometimes years at a stretch, *Sabre*'s amenities included extensive training facilities, gymnasiums, and recreation rooms. Which Lager had convinced Gareth he needed to visit, too.

But now that he was here, lobbing a zee ball back and forth with a long, droplet-shaped paddle, he felt like he should be doing something else. And not just because Lager had ratcheted the arena gravity up to one-point-five, which made for a particularly rigorous workout.

It didn't matter how hard he ran, or how much he sweated; the sound of Osmond Clay's confident chuckle was still ringing in Gareth's ears, and he could see the hesitant expressions of the rest of the Commission when he closed his eyes. He should be touching base with Commission allies right now or sorting through the pile of reports that was waiting for him on his personal feed. He should follow up on that diplomatic situation on Izo, too. And hadn't Lager mentioned something about another possible altercation?

Lager cracked his paddle into the ball, swinging hard

enough to send the thing into a perfect spiral toward the ceiling. The Lieutenant pumped his fist, already celebrating his victory, but Gareth ran for the ball, paddle extended. The ball was falling too fast, but he pushed hard against the increased gravity, lurching into a dive at the last minute so he could hit the ball back to Lager.

Startled, Lager dove for it, but it was too late. The ball sailed past his paddle and bounced back into the wall behind him, where it fell to the floor with a rolling thump.

"Good one, boss." Lager was grinning, his hairline damp with sweat. He stopped to grab his water bottle from the bench.

When Gareth picked himself up off the floor, he found he was grinning, too. He pointed his paddle at Lager. "Don't get complacent just because you got off one decent shot."

"Not everyone's willing to dig their chin into the floor to score a point."

"That's the problem, Lieutenant. That's the problem." Gareth let his eyes catch on the digital clock above the door. "But I should really be getting back to work. Or at least taking my turn in target practice."

Lager gave his paddle a practice whoosh. "That's a solid no. Everyone on this ship takes rec time, except for you. Ten minutes won't cut it."

Gareth grabbed his own water bottle from the bench and took a beat to drink. "I'm not everyone on the ship. I'm the Commander."

"And your soldiers should see that you use your rec time so they feel comfortable using theirs."

That was... a fair point. If Gareth heard one of his soldiers had been training through their rec time, he'd be meeting with that person to find out why. "I dislike it when you're right, Lieutenant."

Lager bent to retrieve the ball, then tossed it up so he could give it an arching serve. "Speaking of rec time, Jim and I are planning a jaunt to one of the Halorin moon resorts next time leave rolls around. You should come."

Gareth sidestepped, intercepted the shot, and smacked the ball back toward the Lieutenant. The impact against the paddle reverberated through his wrist, and he loosened his hold. "I think Jim might resent a third wheel, Lager. Especially one who happens to be your boss."

"So bring a date. It's going to be a party."

"And I'm so good at parties." Gareth avoided them unless it was absolutely necessary. Unless it was a Fleet function, or a fundraiser he couldn't avoid—the Fleet needed a fair amount of financial support to continue operating—he stayed well away.

"You ever talk to Bree?" Lager asked.

The ball struck Gareth in the shoulder and dropped to the floor as he missed a step. At least he caught himself before he face-planted.

He hadn't spoken to his ex-fiancée since she'd stomped out of his life, what was it, three years ago now? Bree had woken him in the dead of night, demanding a shuttle to take her away from *Sabre,* and that'd been that. No calls, no messages, no nothing. He hadn't even run into her in passing, though she lived near his office on Fane. Or she had.

Gareth had known that Bree wasn't the kind of woman who wanted to live on the move. To be fair, most people weren't. Gareth might've grown up on Fleet frigates, but Bree hadn't wanted to live that way. They'd been trying to work out a solution, some kind of compromise, though now he wasn't even sure what that would've been. Gareth couldn't bring himself to use his rec time unless Lager pushed him into it, and he'd used vacation leave only once, when he'd lost his father.

Bree had seen that, and she'd gone running. He couldn't blame her.

Still, her leaving had felt sudden. Most people had the sense not to bring her up, if they even remembered she existed.

Gareth served the ball back to the Lieutenant, cracking it a bit harder than was strictly necessary for a decent serve. "Why do you ask?"

"Only way to score on you, boss." Lager grinned as he hit the ball back to Gareth. "I'm just making conversation. That's what rec time is for. Bonding."

"I see."

They passed the ball back and forth for a few minutes, mercifully dropping the conversation so they could push harder against the extra-heavy grav settings. The clap-and-thunk of the ball, the squeak of their shoes against the floor. It was good, as long as no one tried to bond with him.

Finally, Gareth hit the ball hard enough to bounce it against the ceiling, and Lager's answering slide wasn't enough to keep the volley going. He stood, brushing off his hands, and trotted over to retrieve the ball. "That's the game," he said. "I better hit the showers if I'm going to make my shift in thirty."

Gareth nodded. "Good game, Lieutenant. Let's do it again."

Lager slung his duffel over his shoulder and took a long draw of water, then popped the bottle into a side pocket. "Look, just come on the vacation. Maybe you could get that bounty hunter to join us, you know? What's her name?"

Sloane Tarnish would probably show up on his vacation

with or without an invitation, just to vex him. "You know her name," Gareth said.

If Lager kept smiling like that, his face was going to split down the middle. "Yes, yes I do."

The man was an absolute menace.

"Yes, well, I'd love to see what the media would say about that trip." He could just picture the feeds, and their glee. The guesses they'd make, the conspiracies they'd whip up. Not that he cared much what the feeds reported, but still.

Lager tipped his head to the side, raising an eyebrow. "And I'd love to know why *that* was your first response instead of 'why the hell would I bring a bloody bounty hunter on a romantic vacation, Lieutenant?'"

Gareth frowned. "I don't sound like that."

Lager winked. "Of course not. Just think about it, boss. With or without the bounty hunter. We'd love to have you."

Gareth clapped Lager on the shoulder, then held the door open for him. "Thanks, Lieutenant, but I'll have to pass. Who would I leave in charge, if not you?"

Lager sighed. "And thus, the best of plans die. I'll see you around, boss."

As the Lieutenant disappeared down the corridor, Gareth couldn't help wondering what he *would* do with a vacation, if he ever took one. He certainly got his fill of adventure commanding the Fleet, and if he were honest, Lager's resort plan would probably bore him to tears after the first day. A camping trip, perhaps. He'd always thought it might be interesting to learn how to fish.

Gareth hung his racket on the wall and left the rec space. Vacations were all well and good, but it would no doubt be years before he actually took one. There was always more work to do.

CHAPTER 7

THE MANUAL FOR *Moneymaker*'s systems was heavy in Sloane's lap, its binding spread across both her legs, its pages crumpled and dog-eared and stained from years of use.

And the brick of a book was only the first of three volumes, too. Ships kept the manuals on paper, the introduction said, in case the computer systems ever went out. Smart. She wouldn't have thought of that.

She knew she could search through the digitized book, pick and choose what to read about, but she didn't need to know something specific; she needed to know *everything*.

So while they made their way toward the illegal bounty BRO had found, she sat down in the chair in her cabin, propped her feet up on the bed, and started at page one. The margins were stuffed with notes in three different handwriting styles, one of which may or may not have been Uncle Vin's.

After plodding through five pages in an hour, she got up, wedged the book under her arm, and started out into the hall. She'd take the book up to engineering and look directly at the parts it was discussing.

If nothing else, it'd help keep her awake.

As she passed the rest of the crew quarters, she hesitated outside Alex's door. Which was closed, as per usual these days. Still cradling the book, she knocked, then opened the door without waiting for a response.

Alex was lounging on her bed and flipping through a holo quiz on her fliptab. Her fingers were stained green from those weird cheese-smelling snacks she liked to eat, and the crumbs were tumbling all over her bedspread. Sloane would definitely need to send a cleaning bot in here later. As soon as she figured out how to fix them. Using the manual.

In the middle of the room, a tableau of holo figures spun on a turntable, each of them filled with a different level of color—pink to the knees, purple to the waist, blue to the nose, etcetera. The headline that drifted above the collection of blue-tinged figures read *Which Celebrity Android Are YOU?*

Sloane hadn't done one of these personality quizzes since she was about sixteen, but she thought the amount of color in each figure represented how much Alex's responses related to that particular celebrity android.

"I didn't say come in," Alex said.

Sloane went in anyway. She leaned against the wall, studying the flickering androids. She'd watched a few vids with android actors as a kid, but she didn't recognize all the figures. "You need a project. Come down and help me learn about the engines and stuff."

"I'm an astrophysicist, not a mechanic."

Yeah, yeah. That was Alex's excuse for everything. Sloane had guessed that Vin must have hired the science officer in hopes of supporting her work with wormholes, but his reasons for that were still a mystery. What had Vin wanted to know about wormhole tech?

Maybe he'd just wanted to keep Alex safe.

Sloane squinted at the quiz and the rapidly shifting androids. They were making her dizzy. "According to this, you're actually... Sindy Bolts. Huh. I'd have said Artemis Wrencher."

Sindy specialized in mysteries, where she usually played a detective. Artemis tended to play the guy who supplied the detective with cool tech, or the mad scientist who threatened the world with cool tech. In general, Artemis did stuff with cool tech.

Android actors were weird.

Alex's posture went rigid and she looked up at Sloane with eyebrow-raised offense. "But Wrencher's such a nerd."

"Exactly." Sloane stepped through the android quiz and sat down at the foot of the bed, staying well clear of the green cheese crumbs. "OK, yes, you're an astrophysicist. So what? I'm a doctor. No one cares. Come on, help me learn."

Alex flicked the quiz closed, popped a cheese snack into her mouth, and opened another link. "You're not a doctor yet. Shut the door on the way out, will you?"

Sloane watched her for another minute, but Alex just gave her a pointed look, so she sighed and headed for the door. "You know where to find me if you change your mind."

"I won't."

The crew hallways felt too quiet, with Alex avoiding her lab and Hilda flying. Oliver's door was shut fast, as if she could pretend the lying, backstabbing, ex-kind-of-boyfriend of a security officer had never betrayed her and then died trying to take it back.

As for Uncle Vin's door? She kept that one open.

Uncle Vin hadn't been the kind of uncle who showed up with his pockets stuffed with candy or gifts. No, he'd been the kind of uncle who came with wild tales that little Sloane had only ever half believed, who'd spread system maps on the table and pointed to each place he'd visited, who'd let her play on his spaceship.

And who'd taught her to slip a card up her sleeve in the middle of a high-stakes game.

She'd been about ten, she thought, when Vin had stayed up late into the night to play cards with her father. Her uncle's visits had been sporadic and infrequent, but Dad always agreed to see him. Dad might have called the authorities, reported Vin's presence—his brother was an outlaw, wanted in half the galaxy—but he never did.

Sloane remembered waking up to her father's laughter. Dad was a serious man, not much for riotous laughter, and the sound had drawn her out of bed and into the kitchen. Mom had been in bed, while the two men had a face-card game spread out across the table. They were betting with candy, the bright colored dots piled into a small mountain in the center of the table.

Instead of sending her back to bed, Dad had invited her to join the game. Feeling very grown up, Sloane had gone to sit between them.

"There's a secret to playing cards," Dad had explained. "Strict attention to detail. Every tap of the fingers, every twitch of the eyebrow. It might be a tell, or it might be a bluff. You learn to read the patterns, and you'll win more than you lose."

But Vin scoffed at that. "Your father's only half right. The secret is to know your opponent, and then make your own luck."

Dad sat back in his chair, spreading his palms out wide. "Do tell."

Uncle Vin smiled. He flipped his hands, mimicking Dad's posture, and held his cuffs out for Sloane to see. When Sloane looked at her father, he simply shrugged.

But then Vin had embarked on a lesson, showing Sloane how to distract your opponent so you could slip a high card out of your cuff, how to watch his hand from a hidden camera or even a mirror.

"But you're playing for candy," Sloane said. "Why would you cheat?"

Try as she might, she couldn't recall what her uncle had said. She only remembered that her father had ended the game—or had that been another time?—and lectured her gently about Vin's negative influence as he'd tucked her back into bed. Yes, Dad and Vin were brothers, and no, Dad wouldn't call the authorities or turn him in. But that didn't mean Vin could be trusted.

Right now, with Vin's door standing open and Oliver's shut fast, *Moneymaker*'s crew quarters really did feel like a monument to the men who'd betrayed her. Who would be next?

It wasn't that Vin had betrayed her, at least not in the same way Oliver had. But why had he disappeared, and why had he keyed the ship so it only answered to her? Why leave his crew with his inept niece?

She didn't belong in his world, and Vin had to know it. But he'd shoved her into it, anyway.

Sloane's fingers dug into the edges of the book as she moved past Oliver and Vin's doors, making her way to the spiral staircase. She'd have to rely on herself, now. And that would have to be enough.

CHAPTER 8

THE BEST COURSE OF ACTION, Gareth had decided, would be to head back to Cadence System. He couldn't reason the Commission into helping him with the Federation, so he'd need to cajole the members individually.

And he couldn't host them on *Sabre*. So, Cadence System it was. At least his mother would be glad to get a visit from him.

As *Sabre* headed out of the Adu System, Gareth couldn't help but feel like he was leaving a nest of vipers behind, one that could multiply and infest the entire galaxy. He stood on the bridge, watching through the frigate's enormous viewport as Adu's light faded into the distance, and found himself thinking that the planets and moons in this system were beautiful, and that, infested as they were, they glittered just the same as the planets in any so-called civilized Center System.

The Fleet was supposed to set boundaries between Systems, and they did. But it wasn't just about containing the rot to Adu; it couldn't be. There were innocent people here, and for centuries they'd been subject to the whims of a tyrannical overlord. Now that dictator was gone, yet their lives were still in danger. If they didn't join the crime that festered here, they would eventually succumb to it.

They needed someone to watch over them. If that made him sound a bit self-righteous, even to himself, then so be it.

"Half the Fleet is still in the Bone System, sir. It'll be okay until we return." Lieutenant Lager stood beside Gareth on the bridge, fliptab open in one hand, his other arm tucked into the small of his back. As usual, Lager had an eerie way of knowing what Gareth was thinking. It made him a good Lieutenant. A good friend, too.

Gareth nodded. He'd make a poor commander if he couldn't trust his own people. Still, it tugged at his stomach. It felt like committing a betrayal.

At the edge of the System, the Adu Current streamed by, its sinuous blue-green light curling through the galaxy like a ribbon on a gift. Until recently, Adu System's exits had been off-limits, the Currents programmed to skip the place entirely. Now, though, this portion of the Current network was fair game.

Currents allowed for quick travel through the galaxy, bringing ships to near lightspeed travel while countering the effects of G-forces and relativity. Like most of the non-scientific world, Gareth didn't know the specifics of how they worked; he only knew that Currents facilitated trade and allowed communication to flow through the galaxy in close to real time. Without crushing the human body, or causing time to warp around it.

Sabre was headed for the Adu Current now, and that would put him back in the nearby Cadence System in less than a day. Once there, he'd leverage some connections and call in some favors—he was owed more than a few—to secure a meeting with the Federation.

A petty rivalry was one thing. But the Federation was overstepping, placing bounties on Fleet-classed criminals and sending hunters to interfere with situations that should be solely in his jurisdiction.

Gareth didn't deny the importance of the Federation; trade had to be regulated, and criminals held to account. Allowing worlds to set bounties on criminals was a way to do that.

But though the Federation claimed to take a hands-off approach to conflict and politics, it seemed to Gareth that they regulated too many aspects of galactic trade. They put their own organization in the seat of power, all the while holding themselves as if they were above reproach.

He didn't like it, and he didn't like them. And yet, he needed to set a meeting.

An alert shimmered across the viewport, red letters interrupting his contemplation of the Bone System and the Federation. He wrapped his fingers around the rail, leaning forward slightly. What was this, now?

"Four ships approaching from the rear." Rachel Stills, the officer who reported this, was sitting directly below him. She was typing into a console that extended over her lap, no doubt following the outlined protocol to the letter. "No response to contact attempt."

"Five ships to starboard," another officer said. "No response there either, sir."

Gareth usually hated standing physically above his officers like this, as if he were keeping his distance from the people who did the actual work. In moments like this, though, he understood it; he could see the entire floor, watch all his officers as they leapt into action, and change the images on the viewport at will. It was necessary.

"Transponder signals?" Gareth asked.

"None, sir."

"Got a source for the ships, then?" A ship's trajectory could tell a lot about where it might have come from.

A pause. "Izo."

Gareth glanced at Lager, who was already swiping furiously on his fliptab. On the viewport, a collection of ship models zipped up to obscure the live view out the window, each rotating slowly to reveal its full specifications.

The cartels often thought hiding their ship idents would prevent them from being recognized. More often than not, though, the designs of their vessels were enough to identify them. The slim, vertical rectangles that filled the window now were a giveaway for Callow Clan. It was like being followed by a bunch of sticks.

In contrast, their allies flew fat-bodied ships with so many rail guns and cannons that they looked like a bunch of squarish sea urchins. He had the sudden urge to pluck one of the rectangle ships off the viewport and use it to like a zeeball paddle to send the sea-urchin ships out into the abyss. If only.

Gareth had never been foolish enough to think a smaller ship meant a less powerful one. *Sabre* had all the protections a hulking star frigate could be expected to carry, but small ships could be surprising, and the cartels were nothing if not innovative.

"Lieutenant, didn't you say we brokered an agreement between Callow and Mechic on Izo?" Gareth asked.

Lager was still swiping away on his fliptab. "Yes, sir."

"When you said they were getting along, I thought you meant refraining from killing each other. Not ganging up on *us* together."

"Maybe they're here to thank us," Lager said.

"Guns are hot," Stills said. She hadn't stopped typing.

"And sometimes we do our jobs a little too well," Gareth said.

Lager grimaced. "Yes, sir."

Well. It wouldn't be the first time.

"Missiles incoming," Stills said, though it was hardly necessary; he could see the angry red dots spitting out of the ship models on the viewport.

"Intercept," Gareth said.

On the viewport, *Sabre*'s answering missiles canceled the first round. And then everything was motion as the cartels fired more rounds and *Sabre* fired back.

"Try not to hit them," Gareth said. "Defense only."

He wouldn't have minded knocking their heads together, just a bit, but only enough to shake some sense into the fools. The Fleet had come to *help* them, had negotiated a truce between them, and this was their response.

Still, he wouldn't take them down. Not like this. The cartels might be innovative, but Gareth still commanded the elephant that could squash the ant. Besides, the optics of it would land him in headache-inducing meetings for a month. The Commission liked it that he *had* battle ships, but seemed to prefer he not use them.

Politics, even in the middle of a fight.

Sabre quivered as one of the cartels' missiles evaded its interceptor to strike the frigate. A small hit landed; Gareth might not have even felt it, had he not seen the red mark land on the viewport. But small hits could take down a giant, could they not?

"We're two minutes from Current interception," Lager said. "We could make a run for it."

Gareth shook his head. "They're trying to chase us out of the System. If we retreat now, they'll go after *Cutlass* and *Katana* next."

He wouldn't let the Fleet remain locked out of Adu for another century. This System needed them.

Luckily, the frigate had more than guns at her disposal.

"Are the pilots at their stations?" Gareth asked.

"Yes, sir," Stills confirmed.

"Have them do a stun net. I want this over."

"It'll bring the systems down for a full minute," Lager said.

Gareth shook his head. "It's worth it." He swiped the viewport clean and shifted the cameras so he could watch the cube-shaped fighter pods zip out of their spots along the bottom of the frigate. They locked onto the larger ships in detachable blocks, and they were smaller than the sea-urchin ships that swarmed the frigate like angry bees.

They packed an excellent punch, though. One he was particularly proud of.

As the cartel ships chipped away at *Sabre*'s shields, the cube ships split into two columns. It was happening to the stern and to starboard, a sort of synchronized dance. He'd flown in similar formations himself, dozens of times, but he'd been assigned to larger ships by the time the Fleet had invented the stun nets.

Right about now, the cartels would be laughing at the box-like ships that shot out of the frigate, moving as if to bypass them on either side.

The cube-ships shimmered until thick threads of golden light spun between them, locking them together. *Sabre*'s lights flickered in warning, and the shields snapped to zero. Not Gareth's favorite thing.

Before the enemy ships could take advantage, though, the cubes soared between them, seizing every system that passed between them in a storm of electrical energy.

Their weapons systems would fizzle, and their engines

would die, leaving their ships dead in the water until Gareth willed it—or until they called their friends to help. The beauty of it? The nets left life support systems intact.

"Weapons cold," Stills said.

Gareth let out a breath, and Lager nodded. It was good, when it worked this way. It didn't always. After a tense minute, the shields went live again.

"Comms," Gareth said.

"Open frequency, sir."

Gareth wrapped his fingers around the bridge railing, anchoring himself against the cool metal. "Perhaps next time you might hesitate to attack those who only want to help."

"The Bone System is ours." The voice came back quickly, without even a beat of hesitation. "The Fleet can leave now, or bathe in its own blood."

Lovely. Gareth signaled Stills to close the comms; there was no point in pursuing the conversation at this point.

On the viewport, the cube ships were returning to lock back onto the frigate. The Fleet's real power, in Gareth's view, was to subdue without causing any harm. If others disagreed, well, that was their prerogative.

"Resume path to the Current," Gareth said.

"Yes, sir. But there's another ship approaching." Stills sounded surprised. "It's... it looks like a star cruiser, sir. It just exited the current."

A cruiser? That was the galaxy's equivalent of a yacht, and a fancy one at that. Who was headed into Adu System in a *yacht*? Whoever they were, they'd fall prey to pirates in less than an hour. "Transponder ident?"

Stills bent her head over her console. "It originated from Cappel. Ident says... It's Osmond Clay. He's requesting to come aboard."

Excellent. Exactly what Gareth needed right now. He resisted rubbing his face with his hand—no need to show his soldiers his dread of meeting with a member of the Commission—but it was a near thing.

"Current's right there," Lager said. "Maybe we weren't home."

Gareth sighed. Politics were politics. He'd already blown Clay off once, and the man had responded by coming to him. Might as well take it as a win. "Let him approach. We need to check damages before committing to the Current, anyway. Lager, take command of the bridge."

"Yes, sir." When Gareth turned to go, Lager said, "If I may, sir?"

Friend-to-friend, the man would say whatever he wanted, whether Gareth wanted to hear it or not. On the bridge, though, he was all etiquette and protocol. It seemed strange, at times, though Gareth should be used to it; he'd certainly seen his father's friends slide between the two roles as a matter of course.

"Go on," Gareth said.

Lager nodded. "Don't meet him at the airlock. Make him come to you."

A wise man, Lager.

Twenty minutes later, Gareth met Osmond Clay in a conference room on the mid-level of the ship. Clay had a glass of amber-colored liquid in front of him, though Gareth hadn't instructed anyone to provide such a refreshment. What did the man do, carry it around in his pocket?

Gareth settled himself at the head of the table. Round tables might be all well and good for the Commission, but he was the leader here. "What can I do for you?"

Clay chuckled and raised his glass in a toast. "I got the

message, Commander. Loud and clear. You don't like a summons. So I came to you, out of respect."

Gareth prided himself in keeping his expression neutral. At least, as much as that was possible for anyone. "What is it, Clay?"

Clay set his glass on the table and leaned his forearms on the edge, imitating Gareth's posture. His wide sleeves dipped over the side of the table, practically falling to his lap. "I need your help."

Obviously he wanted something, though whether he needed actual help remained to be seen. "Oh?"

Clay licked his lips and grimaced, as if the words he needed to say tasted sour. "I've got an employee who stole millions of tokens in data chips from my factory. Just made off with them in the night. I need to... retain him."

Cappel was a famously guarded System, and Gareth didn't know much about their security protocols. Either something had been seriously lacking, or the thief had been very good.

Regardless, it wasn't a job for the Fleet. "I'm not an errand boy, Clay. You must have people for that sort of thing."

Surely he could find some of their ilk right here in Adu. Not that Gareth condoned that. The best course of action, the usual course, would be to reach out to the Federation and arrange a bounty posting.

Clay cringed. "I can't let my bruisers—don't make that face, Fortune, you know what they are—know that it's so easy to rob the facility. We're upping the security, but in the meantime, I need... discretion."

Gareth just stared at him. Apparently, his stony expression needed some work. Or Clay just had a read on him. The man didn't lack intelligence.

"I'd be grateful," Clay added. "It's rather embarrassing."

Certainly. So why would Clay expect Gareth to keep his embarrassing secret for him? It was almost suspect, except that Gareth had to concede that he'd established a reputation for honest discretion. He wanted the Fleet to be trusted, not feared, though this wasn't exactly the situation he had in mind.

Still, he had ships to run, soldiers to feed, and an abandoned System to contain. "How grateful?" he asked.

Clay tsked. "How mercenary of you, Fortune. Half a million data chips for the Fleet, then, and my eternal thanks."

Gareth nodded. He wouldn't apologize for keeping his ships running. "And a meeting with the Cosmic Trade Federation."

"What makes you think I can—"

"The meeting, or you're on your own," Gareth interrupted. "Like I said, Clay, I'm not an errand boy, and I'm not a bounty hunter. But I do have a Fleet to fund."

Clay held up his hands. "Fine. I'll do what I can."

"Then I'll do what I can. Send me the particulars."

"You'll need to track the man. I've no idea where he is."

"Not a problem."

Clay drained the last of his drink and stood. When he reached the door, he paused and turned back, a half-smirk on his lips. It was a snake of a smile, sharp and venomous and far from friendly. "Interesting how you say you don't like politics, Fortune. I'd say you're pretty damn good at them."

With that, he made his way into the hall, letting the door slam behind him and leaving Gareth to wonder when he'd mentioned his dislike of politics where Osmond Clay could hear.

CHAPTER 9

IT WASN'T that Sloane had expected an illegal bounty to
be hiding out in a pleasant spot. She couldn't have hoped to
pick them up at a lux station in the Bone System—there
were no lux stations in the Bone System, that she knew of—
or a penthouse apartment.

Still, she thought it was fair to wish for a bit less mud.

Cal Cornum was the second rock from Adu, the System
star, though Sloane thought the word 'rock' might be giving
the planet a bit too much credit. Every step left her ankle-
deep in mud, and as thankful as she was for her knee-high
boots, she suspected this muck would soak through them
soon enough.

Worse than that, the place smelled like a garbage heap
full of rotten fruit. With a generous dose of sulphur added
in, for good measure. The air was thick and muggy, and the
foul smells curdled on the back of her tongue with every
breath she took.

She'd brought both Alex and Hilda along for this particular adventure, leaving Brighton in BRO's care. Which
didn't seem like the best idea, but there wasn't much she

could do about it. She needed people on the ground with her, especially for a job like this one.

Alex and Hilda were both muttering under their breaths as they followed her through the jungle. She couldn't really blame them for that.

"Don't worry," Sloane said, "I'm going to raise both your salaries."

As soon as she could pay them anything, she would.

"Save my cut for Vincent's rescue fund," Hilda said. "He can pay me back later."

With interest, Sloane assumed.

"Cal Cornum was never terraformed!" BRO informed her as she struggled her way through the jungle. She'd fitted a button-sized bud into her ear so the AI could advise her, though so far it'd only offered tour-guide-level facts about the place. "It was always like this! Isn't that amazing!"

"Yeah, fabulous," Sloane said. "Do you have a dial-back feature on the exclamation points?"

"No!"

The bounty posting BRO had lifted from the Fox Clan databases was very particular about locating the target on Cal Cornum, even providing approximate coordinates. Sloane had to admit she hadn't seen all that many bounties in the short life of her career so far, but the ones she *had* seen never specified a location. Hence the need for a hunter to do the work.

But this was an illegal bounty, and a whole different game. Besides, she could understand why someone with tokens to spare might hire out a job like this instead of enduring a festering boil of a planet like Cal Cornum. Even the trees looked sick, each of them littered with human-sized leaves that dragged their branches toward the ground.

More like pods than leaves, actually, some of them dripping a pus-like substance into the mud.

"Why would this guy come here with a load of stolen data chips?" Sloane asked. "It seems like the humidity would damage the tech."

"Maybe he stashed them somewhere else and he's just hiding out here." Hilda stepped around a fallen chunk of one of the leaf-pods, carefully avoiding the puddle of pus that pooled all around it.

"BRO, can you see if there are any communication signals leaving the planet from this area?" Sloane asked. "Maybe he's going to meet with a buyer."

What else would he do with all those data chips? There had to be thousands of potential buyers in the Galaxy, people who would pass the chips through criminal networks or change up their coding, so they looked legitimate. She'd get into that game herself, if she could figure out how.

"No communication signals," BRO said. "Wait, there is one! It's right near where you're—oh, that *is* you. Apologies."

Hilda sighed.

Sloane pushed a pair of leaf-pods aside, struggling past the tree and into a clearing that was carpeted in a thick layer of sickly green moss. A ring of tall grasses encircled the clearing, as if it meant to spring a trap.

Ahead, the jungle thickened again and led up a steep hill. She squinted, using her sleeve to wipe stinging sweat out of her eyes. At the top of the hill, she could make out a black-sided tower, looming ominously over the jungle. It ended in a jagged spire, though, the stone crumbling away. "Is that a tower?"

"Yes!" BRO said. "Those are the Cal Cornum ruins! No

one knows that was here when it was built, but the stone has been dated back a thousand years! Isn't that amazing!"

On another day, the almost-art-history major in Sloane might have wanted to dig into the jungle or rocket up the hill to check out the ruins. Maybe there'd been a city here, some ancient hub of civilization. Maybe it'd been here long before they'd been able to connect with the rest of the galaxy, or even the System. Maybe long before the Bone System had fallen under the rule of tyranny.

On another day, she'd have her fliptab out, and she'd be asking BRO to tell her everything it could find. Today, she just wanted to collect this guy—his name was Jackson Bellow, according to the posting—and get the hell off this planet.

"Yeah," Sloane said. "So I bet he's there. Good vantage point. Is there any chance you can get a read on those chips?"

"Yes!" BRO said. "There are enabled data chips in the ruins! Hundreds of them!"

Hilda grunted. "The guy didn't even disable the chips? Sloane, either he's a complete amateur, or this is some kind of a trap."

If it was a trap, it was too late. They were already here. Jackson Bellow was a turncoat factory employee with no criminal record. She could imagine a person like that being inept at criminal undertakings or getting caught in a black-mail situation. Not that she planned to play the hero here.

"Let's hope it's the first," Sloane said. "Come on, this is going to be easy."

Something struck her hard in the back, and she fell face-forward into the mud. If it'd smelled bad before, it was absolutely rancid as it oozed up her nostrils. She twisted, flailing for her pistol, but her hands were slippery, and the gun went flying.

"Move!" Hilda shouted, and Sloane scrambled through the mud as something large and squelchy thundered behind her. She stumbled to her feet, nearly losing her footing again as she risked a glance back over her shoulder.

The thing that had hit her in the back looked like a huge slimy log that suddenly decided to go for a stroll. A slimy log with slimy wings that it now extended as it staggered around, like a colt testing its legs. At its feet—or the base of the log, since she didn't *see* any feet—one of the heavy leaves from the tree had cracked open.

The leaves weren't leaves, and they weren't pods, either. They were cocoons, and one of them had birthed this... thing, whatever it was. To either side, its brothers writhed in their cocoons, ready to break free. The first monster sprang into the tree and startled rustling around, dragging its drenched wings through the actual foliage. Drying them? Scratching an itch?

Sloane didn't realize she'd stopped moving to gape until Alex's fingers closed around her arm to drag her across the rest of the clearing and into the jungle ahead. It was hard to say what good that would do, but the monster was still cracking those curdled wings against the tree, so it was as good a plan as any.

Leaving her pistol in the mud, Sloane fled after Alex, who'd picked up a stick at some point—it looked like a cousin to the cocoon monster—and looked ready to impale it if she had to. Only Sloane wasn't convinced any stick would break that thing's carapace.

"BRO," Sloane said, breathing hard as she started up the jungle-enclosed incline toward the ruins, "what *are* those things?"

"No idea!" BRO answered cheerfully.

"Alex?"

"By all means, let's stop to perform a full analysis. After I remind you that I'm not a biologist, I'm an *astrophysicist*."

A branch struck Sloane across the forehead, and she lost her footing, landing on her ass in the mud. She kicked uselessly as the slop soaked into her pants, until Hilda wheeled back to offer her a hand.

By now, though, the slime monster had crossed the clearing in two pumps of its massive wings. It followed them straight into the trees, its log-face gaping. It was still dripping with cocoon pus. "I think we smell like something it wants to eat," Sloane said.

Hilda had managed to keep a hold on her gun—a hand cannon that Sloane hadn't seen before; the pilot must've picked it up on Shard—and she raised it now, bracing the heels of her hands against the handle as she shot a round into what she guessed was the creature's stomach.

The slime monster wheeled back, wings flailing as smoke churned out of its middle. It let out a horrific screech, and Sloane didn't stop to see if it was dead, or if its friends had gotten the message; she followed Hilda up a short rise, to where a set of crumbling stone steps switchbacked up to the top of the hill.

When they reached the ruins, they dove inside, Alex on their heels. If only there were a door to close or a moat to hide behind.

There wasn't, but it didn't matter; the creatures hadn't followed. Maybe the hand cannon had scared them off. Or maybe their wings needed to dry more—good luck, in this place—before they could fly higher.

Flying slime monsters. Not a pretty thought.

Whatever the reason, the screeches died away, and

Sloane stood with her back against the black wall of the broken tower, desperately attempting to draw air into her lungs. When she peered out of the stone-bordered archway, she could see the jungle canopy in crisp detail, except for a lace of mist that drifted by in the distance. A pair of birds took off from a tree near the clearing, chittering, but there was no sign of any slime monsters, even when Sloane enhanced the focus on her eye screen.

"Thank you for making me a part of this," Alex said. She was half-crouched next to Sloane, head dropped between her knees.

A shadow flinched in Sloane's peripheral vision, and she reached for her pistol before she realized she'd dropped it in the mud. Hilda had it covered, though; she withdrew the hand cannon and pointed it toward the man who'd emerged from deep within the ruined building.

He was thin and bald, with pale skin and puffy lips that were surprisingly large for his smallish face. "Oh," he said. "What took you so long?"

"That's him!" BRO said in Sloane's ear. "Jackson Bellow! Your bounty!"

Sloane frowned at the man. "What do you mean?"

"Where's your ship?" Bellow stuck his hands on his hips, and he spoke in a tone that was tinged with annoyance, articulating his words with a note of condescension that made her want to punch him. "You were supposed to extract me. That would require a ship."

Sloane stared at him, as though his face might provide some explanation. Usually, bounties went running the other way. They didn't rebuke you for lack of planning. "What kind of mushrooms have you been licking in this jungle?" she asked.

"What... Oh." The man scratched his head. "You're not in on it. Huh."

"In on *what?*"

"Sloane." Hilda spoke from the arch, and Sloane turned to follow the pilot's gaze out over the jungle.

In the clearing they'd just been chased out of, a quartet of Fleet soldiers stomped their way through the mud toward the hill. Much more easily, she noticed, than she had; not one of them sank as far as their ankles. Not fair.

When she zoomed her eye screen view in close, she could see the soldiers had traded their pretty midnight-blue uniforms for light armor. She could also see that Commander Fortune was with them. Because of course he was.

And in the tree those squawking birds had just abandoned, she could see the barest glint of a hand-cannon barrel, peeking out of the trees and aiming straight for the Fleet soldiers.

Hilda had been right; the bounty was definitely a trap. Only it hadn't been set for Sloane.

CHAPTER 10

GARETH DOUBTED there were many men who would say Cal Cornum was a pleasant place for a ground operation. It was muddy and humid, with mosquitos in the air and a rotting odor that he suspected would take days to get out of his nostrils.

In truth, though, he'd seen worse. The light armor kept him relatively cool, and it made trudging through the muck a slightly easier task. Heavy armor would've taken him down to his knees, and he doubted he'd need that much firepower today.

Leaving Lager in charge on *Sabre*, Gareth had recruited four officers to help him secure Osmond Clay's rogue employee. He didn't like sending soldiers to ground for an operation he himself hesitated to accept at all, so it felt right to join them.

An itch between his shoulder blades told him there was more to this job than Clay had admitted. Gareth shouldn't have taken it, but the allure of a meeting with the Federation was too great to ignore. And the Fleet needed those data chips, rather desperately.

As the thought crossed his mind, something pattered through the canopy above him, flicking the leaves a touch too hard for seeds or raindrops.

"Under fire!" one of the soldiers shouted.

A light flashed up in the canopy, accompanied by a loud boom that could only come from one type of weapon.

And then someone slammed into him from the right, knocking him onto his side and sending him sliding through the mud and into a patch of long grass. Shots rang out in the jungle as his soldiers returned the fire that rained down through the trees at them. How many hand cannons were up there?

Gareth tried to get up, but his attacker pushed him back down. He could have shaken her off with one hand, but some instinct made him refrain. She didn't pull a gun or a knife; instead, she dropped to the mud beside him, keeping one hand on his back as if to prevent him from rising.

"Why are you wearing this bullshit armor, Fortune?" she said. "That suit couldn't stop a sewing needle."

Gareth blinked the mud out of his eyes. Sloane Tarnish. She was covered in dirt, but she was unmistakable, with that long chestnut hair. Most bounty hunters kept their locks short or braided them into coils. Not Sloane. She'd just tied it back at the nape of her neck, inviting any villain to seize it. She was either exceedingly confident or very, very green.

Given her recent appearance on the scene, he was inclined to think she was both. But what the hell was she doing *here*?

"You're not wearing *any* armor," he said.

She waved him away, like he was a mere annoyance, and not the Commander of the entire Galactic Fleet. "I'm not exactly flush with tokens. Stay *down*, Fortune. The bounty I came for was expecting me to drive his getaway ship, and he was definitely expecting *you*. This was a setup. Your soldiers know to take cover, so you need to do it, too."

She was right. He'd been ready to get up, to find his people, but they were well trained. Better than he was, perhaps; they'd taken cover in the trees, hiding behind those massive, teardrop-shaped leaves, and were trading shots with the snipers in the canopy ahead.

Clay had set him up, then. Of course he had. But why? It was a bold move, and it felt like a clumsy one. If they pinned an assassination attempt on him, he'd be ousted from the Commission. His entire system would be subject to a raid. The man could lose everything.

"I'll ping my ship," Gareth said.

Sloane touched his wrist. "And if that's what they're hoping for? He's got the high ground up there. He might have hand cannons ready."

"Hand cannons can't take down a Fleet frigate."

"And a Fleet frigate can't blow up the whole jungle without taking you out with it. This situation calls for a little finesse, Fortune."

Because she was the poster-girl for finesse. Gareth sighed. "All right, what do you propose?"

She stared into the tree line. It wasn't far; if he could stand without fear of getting shot, he'd be there in five steps. "Did that bullshit armor come with a knife?" she asked.

"If it did, should I hand it over to a random bounty hunter?"

Sloane held out a hand, palm up. "If she just saved your life, then yes, you should."

Gareth contemplated her for a moment. She was covered in grime, but that spark in her eyes said she had a plan. Sloane Tarnish might have shown herself to be deceitful, and often mercenary, but he didn't think she was the kind of woman who'd save his life just to murder him. If anything, she'd risked her own life by crashing down here when she could have simply collected her bounty and left.

Gareth loosened a blade from his hip and handed it to her. "Am I going to regret this?"

"Probably." Sloane grinned—was the damn woman *enjoying* this?—and started to crawl, dragging her body through the mud and leaving an indented trail that immediately filled with dirty water. "Come on, Fortune. We're going to have to run."

She had the same gleam in her eyes that'd been there when she'd handed him her glass of champagne back on Shard. Gareth didn't see any gravity anchors or hov-train channels here, but if Sloane knew something he didn't, he'd just have to trust her.

A frightening thought.

Sloane crawled straight to the tree line. His soldiers were still on the other side of the clearing, at his back, but Gareth didn't want to reveal his location by pinging them through the comms. Sloane's side of the clearing was dripping with just as many of those enormous leaves, and he had trouble believing they made good cover for his soldiers. He hoped no one had been hurt.

When Sloane reached the tree line ahead, she turned and pressed a finger to her lips.

And then she leapt to her feet, knife at the ready. She plunged it into the nearest hanging pod and dragged it across the thing's yellow-green wall. Limbs tumbled out of the pod with a gush, soaking her head in a layer of thick fluid—there were *animals* in there, or some kind of giant insect—but Sloane kept running, piercing one leaf after another to spill the fleshy contents onto the jungle floor.

"Run, Fortune," she shouted, still slashing, "up to the ruins!"

"I don't see what—"

At the end of the row, the first pod animal—he didn't know what they were, or what to call them—rose on shaky legs, extending a pair of wings that doubled the span of his own arms. Which a screech, it leapt into the canopy to crash among the branches.

Abruptly the shooting stopped, replaced by the terrified screams of the sniper who'd been targeting them from that tree. Gareth didn't know if these creatures would attack the snipers, but they could certainly scare them away.

Gareth paused at the tree line to open his comm, signaling his soldiers to make their way through the clearing.

Sloane grabbed his wrist and hauled him toward the cut-up section of mud that told him she'd come this way before. "You need to work on your self-preservation instincts," she said. "Those things will dry their wings and drop back down, and then they'll come for us. Come on!"

Gareth didn't know how she could possibly know that, but there was no denying her knack for acquiring obscure information.

He wasn't foolish enough to disregard her warning. With his soldiers on their heels, each of them scanning the trees for hidden assailants, he let her drag him up the hill to a set of crumbling steps. "Can I tell my ship to extract us now?" he asked.

"Of course not." She darted under the black stone entrance to the ruins, her fingers locked tightly around his wrist. "I've still got a bounty to catch."

CHAPTER 11

"YOU'VE STILL GOT a *bounty* to catch?" Fortune's tone was one Sloane had heard from many people during her thirty-plus years of life. Disbelief mixed with offense that often bordered on outrage, though Fortune mostly just sounded surprised.

Okay, maybe a little annoyed. But not outraged.

She kept a hold on his wrist as she dove into the blackened ruins, for no reason other than that she was pretty sure he wouldn't let her die if someone popped up and tried to kill her. He was righteous that way. Good to keep someone like that close.

"I'm not getting paid to extract you, Fortune." Her breaths were coming with difficulty, her lungs fighting all the running and climbing and slashing. She was covered in that monster cocoon goo, and her scalp was starting to sting. She really hoped the stuff wasn't poisonous.

"If anything, they might try to kill you, too," he said.

They could try. "I cannot lose this bounty," she said. "I am turning him in. I am getting the tokens. And I am finishing this mission."

The words crossed her lips like a mantra, as if she could somehow will Jackson Bellow and his supposedly stolen data chips to still be here. Would the bounty posters still pay her, after she'd messed up their true plan?

They would. They had to. She'd *make* them. She wasn't sure how, but she would. Uncle Vin would get them to.

She'd promised Hilda. No more side trips, no more distractions. Fix the ship. Find Vin. Without this bounty, they would only be delayed again.

She started forward, readying her knife, and wishing for her pistol, but Fortune tugged her back. "Slow down." He gestured to his soldiers. "Clear the ruins."

The soldiers pressed their guns into their shoulders and started dipping through the crumbling doorways, peering around corners, and barking reports of 'clear' back and forth.

Right. Clear the ruins. Good call.

"BRO," Sloane said, "can you get *Moneymaker* down here?"

Fortune was blinking at her like he was trying to piece together why she'd just called him 'bro.' Which would have been funny, if she could be at all certain that was what he was thinking. He was still eighty-five percent inscrutable, even with his plastic-mask expression covered in a layer of dirt and slime, and his bullshit armor sporting a new design of muddy wet grass.

Somehow, she thought he wore the look much better than she did. He looked rugged, while she probably looked like one of those cocoon monsters. With a ponytail.

"Yes!" BRO said. "I can get *Moneymaker* down here!"

"Where are Alex and Hilda?"

"Hiding!" BRO said.

Good. That was good. They should stay out of danger. Sloane let go of Fortune's wrist and took a step forward.

"Wait," Fortune said. "Give my soldiers a chance to clear the—"

A figure leapt down from the closest wall and slammed into Sloane, knocking her sideways and into the stone ruins. Her head bashed into the rock, and stars screamed across her vision as a warm metal blade pressed into her neck. She struggled, trying to force a knee into a groin or an elbow into a throat, but he was holding her too tightly, his bony hip pinning her thigh.

The guy's face wouldn't sink into focus—her vision was spinning, making him a kaleidoscope of skin and nostrils and lips—but she knew it was Bellow. He'd looked too much like a stick to be a threat, but appearances were clearly deceiving. Now that he'd attacked, he was all wiry muscle, his grip as strong as a vise.

"Sorry, girl," he said. "A deal's a deal."

As if she knew what that meant.

And here she'd thought the Commander would be a gentleman and save her life. She was definitely going to become a ghost so she could come back and haunt him.

This was *not* how she'd wanted to die.

But just as the notion flickered through her darkening thoughts, the pressure against her neck eased up. One moment, the blade was pressed into her throat, primed to rip her open. And the next, her attacker was jerking away from her. She couldn't see what had wrenched him away, but she heard the thump as he hit the ground. The air smelled like electricity and ozone, and the hair on her arms stood on end. Something electrical, then. Was the guy still breathing? Did she care?

Sloane squeezed her eyes shut, and her knees gave out,

dropping her against the wall. Her head felt swollen, her thoughts were as fuzzy as her vision, and her neck was sore. Why was her neck sore?

Commander Fortune's face materialized in front of her. It was blurry, but for once his expression was readable. His lips were parted, his gray eyes wide as moons, and the color had drained out of his face. At least, what she could see of his face through the layer of mud. The man was plainly concerned.

No, not concerned. He was *afraid*.

Took a head injury for her to read the man. He should really work on that.

"I suppose you're going to take him from me," she said. Her words sounded slurred. That couldn't be good.

Fortune had been the one to subdue the bounty, so the man really *did* belong to him. Those were the rules. Maybe if she explained, if she told him about the broken ship, about Uncle Vin... But her tongue felt thick in her mouth, and the words wouldn't come together, and she couldn't help thinking it would be really annoying if she died *now*.

Fortune crouched in front of her, peering into her eyes like he was checking for a concussion. Which was probably a good idea, since she was pretty sure she had one. He touched a fingertip to her neck, applying gentle pressure. She must be bleeding, but she couldn't feel it. She wasn't dead, though, so how bad could it be?

"No," he said, and his voice sounded distant, like an echo. "You're going to turn him into the Federation. And I'm going with you."

Oh, she thought, *he thinks it was a Federation-approved bounty*.

And that was the last thought that crossed her mind before the world turned black.

CHAPTER 12

LIEUTENANT LAGER LOOKED UNCOMFORTABLE. His face was scrunched in an expression of disapproval. Almost as if his muscles weren't used to bending that way, which made sense; Lager was usually cheerful, or at least calm and businesslike. He was a flickering hologram in Gareth's palm, his face hardly bigger than a thumbnail, but it was more than clear that he didn't like this plan.

After carrying Sloane to *Moneymaker*'s infirmary, Gareth had been escorted—practically *shoved*—into an empty cabin by Hilda, the pilot. She'd told him not to move, or touch anything, until he'd showered, then added that she had first dibs on the shower and that Alex would be next.

Gareth had given her the coordinates to a mechanic he knew, a guy who worked out of a station at the edge of the Adu System. He wasn't honest enough for the Center or Middle Systems, but he owed Gareth a favor. He'd fix the ship without screwing anything up and get them moving again.

As soon as they were underway, Gareth put in a call to Lager, who proceeded to lecture him on what it was like to receive a squad of soldiers back on the frigate without their Commander. Even after Gareth explained his plan to visit the Federation with Sloane when she turned in her bounty, Lager's expression didn't relax.

Sometimes Gareth questioned who was really in charge here.

"Why don't you stay on *Sabre*?" Lager asked. "We can follow her to the Trade Federation from a close distance."

"I don't trust her not to bolt," Gareth said.

"Where could she possibly go, with a Fleet frigate escorting her? Her ship would fit in our kitchen, sir."

Where would most people go with a Fleet frigate escort? Nowhere. But this was Sloane Tarnish. The woman would find a crevice, a loophole, or a monster in a chrysalis, and she'd be gone before he could begin to guess which way she meant to go.

Osmond Clay had tried to kill him. At the same time, Sloane had come to pick up the man who'd been waiting there to act as Gareth's bait. Gareth didn't fully understand the connection, not yet, but he couldn't wait while the Commission hemmed and hawed over getting him a meeting. Especially when Osmond Clay was clearly in the thick of this whole thing.

Gareth needed to speak with the Federation. Now. "I still want eyes on her," he said.

"We have people for those kinds of jobs," Lager argued. "Your soldiers? Heard of them?"

"I don't want to divert too many resources."

"*You* are a resource, Commander."

Gareth very nearly laughed. "Anyone could do my job, Lager."

"Then why is Osmond Clay trying to assassinate you?"

"Out of an abundance of spite, perhaps?"

"All the more reason to proceed with caution, sir."

Now that Lager had brought up the assassination attempt, though, Gareth could see the truth of the Lieutenant's disapproval. That was fear in the press of Lager's lips, and the rest of the soldiers would be feeling it, too. Gareth would be a fool to ignore that, even if there were no cause for concern.

And in this case, their feelings were well founded. An underhanded attack on the Fleet, presumably by a member of the Commission? It was unprecedented. Rumors would be circulating, and he needed to do what he could to staunch them.

Gareth did his best to lighten his expression, and the tone of his voice, though he wasn't sure how well Lager could even see him through the layer of mud that still coated his face. "I understand your concern, Lieutenant. I'm taking precautions, I promise. And for all her faults, Sloane Tarnish did save my life."

Likely his soldiers' lives, too.

Lager looked at him for a long moment, his raised eyebrows broadcasting his doubt. For all his jokes about inviting Sloane to join them on a vacation, he clearly didn't trust her. "We have people for this, sir," he repeated.

"But none of them are me."

Lager threw up his hands. He knew a lost cause when he heard one. "Fine. But I'm keeping *Sabre* close."

"I'm counting on it, Lieutenant. Keep her in stealth unless I make the call. No need for Ms. Tarnish to know you're on her heels."

"Yes, sir."

Gareth ended the call and brushed his hands on his pants, more for something to do with his hands than because it would clean them. If anything, the motion only made them dirtier. He was still wearing the light armor, and flakes of dried mud scattered onto the floor whenever he moved. He had a feeling Hilda wouldn't appreciate that.

The cabin had clearly been occupied recently. Even without touching anything—Gareth knew when to follow orders—the room told its stories. A sleeve flopping out of a bottom drawer, a dog-eared book on the nightstand. But there was also a thin layer of dust covering the book, as if it hadn't been moved in a while. The place smelled... not musty, exactly; the air cyclers would take care of that. But it still felt stale, as if the fresh air had been locked out for some time.

He knew that Sloane's uncle, Vincent Tarnish, had gone missing. But somehow, this didn't seem like the famous outlaw's room. It was too sparse to belong to a man who'd lived and worked on this ship for decades. If it didn't belong to Vincent, though, then whose was it?

The door cracked open, and Hilda stuck her head in. "Shower's yours. Please use it immediately. Also, we're docking in five."

"Thank you." Gareth hesitated, but his curiosity overcame his reserve. "Whose room is this?"

Hilda shook her head, her damp braid thumping against her back. "Belonged to a dead man. See you in a few, Commander."

He wanted to ask how Sloane was faring in the infirmary, but the pilot was already gone, no doubt heading up to guide the ship into the station. He followed her out the door to find the showers.

After he'd cleaned up and checked in on his mechanic friend—the man had been nearly doubled over with laughter over the state of Sloane's ship—Gareth had forced himself to lie down on the bed in his cabin and close his eyes. He wasn't sure he'd be able to sleep, but he'd try.

He woke several hours later, when the ship deposited the clothes he'd been wearing under his light armor—blue slacks and a white T-shirt—through a port in the wall. Cleaned and pressed. At least that part of the ship was working. He wouldn't have expected *Moneymaker* to have such amenities at all, but it was a relief not to have to borrow a dead man's clothing. He hadn't relished the thought of opening those drawers.

Gareth dressed and stepped into the hall to find the ship was dark and quiet. There were crew quarters here, and a large room at the end of the hall which, when he peeked inside, appeared to be some kind of a lab. But it gave him the same uneasy feeling as his quarters, as if it hadn't been touched in weeks.

When he made his way up to the main deck, he paused at the back viewport, where the blue-green streak of a Current streaked by. How long had he been asleep? Hilda ought to have woken him.

Though then again, Gareth was not Hilda's Commander. He'd do well to remember that.

He made his way down to the infirmary, intending to check in on Sloane. He hadn't quite realized it was where he was headed, but the light was on, and there was truly no reason not to knock.

"I'm decent," Sloane's voice said when he did. "At least, clothing wise."

He smiled, suppressed it, and stepped inside.

Sloane was lying on a cot in the center of the room, her arms slipped through a pair of vital-reading rings that suggested she still had nano-healers in her system. Keeping an eye on that concussion, most likely. She'd freed her hair from the ponytail, and the long dark strands ran over her shoulders like a waterfall. Her arms were bare, revealing light red scratches on her upper arms. She had bandage on her neck, too, taped over the spot where Jackson Bellow had almost slit her throat.

"Oh," she said. "I didn't know you were still here."

"Sorry to disappoint." He took a seat on a stool by the bed. "You've got good med equipment."

"Yeah, well I'm studying medicine. Or I *was*. Can't have subpar supplies when you're chasing people who want to poke holes in you all the time. But you *can* have a ship that doesn't run." She grimaced. "Not always straight on my priorities."

"It runs," Gareth said. "We're in the Current."

Sloane's back snapped straight, eyes widening. "*Money-maker* can't handle the Currents," she said. "The whole ship's going to—"

Gareth held up a hand. "I had it fixed."

Sloane sat back, studying him with hard brown eyes. He'd met her father, on several occasions. Zander was a government officer on Elter, an important man, and though Gareth wasn't sure of his exact job description, he knew that Zander worked with the Commission representative. With, not for.

Zander had called Gareth personally, though, after the incident at the Fleet ball last year. He'd apologized for Sloane's behavior, and Gareth remembered thinking it was strange that the man seemed to think his daughter was a party girl who loved to play pranks. To Gareth, she'd seemed more like an apprentice to a dangerous outlaw.

"I'm not paying you back for the repairs," Sloane said. "Consider it a thanks for saving your life. And before you say you saved my life, too, mine wouldn't have been in danger if I hadn't saved yours first."

"I wasn't going to say that."

She shrugged, dropping her gaze to the blanket and flicking at the seam with her fingernail. "Tell me," she said, "why's the Fleet turning poor scared civilian ships away from Olton Moon? I thought you meant to help people, not frighten them to death."

Gareth blinked. The change of subject felt sudden, and he tried to think of what she could possibly mean. "Olton Moon? In Adu System?"

"Where else? Don't act innocent, Fortune. We were trying to avoid a fight, and we tried to land there, but we got chased away by a bunch of Fleet ships."

Gareth shook his head, slowly. "They must have just looked like Fleet ships."

She rolled her eyes, then grimaced as if the motion had hurt her head. "I know a Fleet cube-ship when I see one. Who else flies those things?"

No one. But it wasn't possible. "Did you check their transponders?"

"I was a little busy trying not to get murdered."

The Fleet kept their ground bases strictly to the Cadence System. Even there, they only had three. It was among the most important guidelines the Commission imposed on them; the Fleet couldn't establish a base in any other System, ever, without first being asked to do so. They couldn't even seek permission.

It didn't matter if the planet or a moon, or a sliver of asteroid. They couldn't even build a station. They could fly their frigates, they could work to keep order, but they could not put long-term boots on the ground without a direct request.

During Gareth's tenure with the Fleet, that request had come in exactly once. And after they'd completed the mission, they'd dismantled the base and retreated.

"We don't have any bases in Adu," he said.

She stared at him, disbelief plain in her eyes. "Fine," she said. "Don't tell me."

Even if he did have a secret base in Adu, he wouldn't disclose it. She couldn't expect him to. But there was nothing to tell.

Clearly, she wasn't going to buy that. "Any other questions for me?" he asked.

He'd meant it as a joke, but she dropped the blanket and leaned forward. "Yeah. What was that weapon you used to take down the bounty on Cal Cornum?"

A much easier question. He hadn't realized she'd been conscious enough to notice it. "Stun cable," he said. "It wraps around the target, immobilizes and disables them with a mild electrical current. It's supposed to act as a tranquilizer."

She nodded. If she was holding the secret-base thing against him, she didn't show it. The woman was a mystery. "That's handy. It's funny, I don't think I've ever been that close to death before."

He set his palms on his thighs, trying not to show his amusement. "The captain of the *Cutlass* reported that you crawled through the barrel of a plasma rail gun to escape that prison station in Adu after Brighton and his associate turned on you."

He wouldn't have believed it had it not been corroborated by an entire ship's worth of soldiers. They'd seen it happen.

"Yeah," she replied. "But the gun wasn't even hot.

This..." She swallowed. "This was a knife to my artery. It's different."

Like the difference between standing on the bridge of a frigate and dodging gunfire in the jungle. Yes, he understood what she meant.

"Is that a thank you?" Gareth asked.

"No. And you haven't thanked *me*."

Hadn't he? "Well," he said, "thank you."

Sloane held his gaze for a long moment, as if she could read every thought, as if she could catalogue every single one of the emotions that he worked so hard to control. No man could manipulate all his body language—it wasn't possible—but where it was within his control, he did so.

With Sloane, it hardly seemed to matter.

She dropped her hands to her sides, transferring her grip to the sheet underneath her. Getting restless, perhaps. A woman like her wouldn't enjoy staying immobile for long.

The cuffs around her wrists beeped, instructing her to relax her hands. "Who's trying to kill you, anyway?" she asked. "And what are you doing joining your soldiers on the ground in nothing but bullshit armor?"

"It's not bullshit," he said. "It's triple-layered fiber tech. It's moveable, protects from the elements, and adds three times the strength to any blow."

"And those bullets would have pierced through it like butter."

"People aren't supposed to have *hand cannons*."

Laws might differ throughout the galaxy, but like the Fleet's restriction from building bases, that one was fairly uniform. Even the Fringe Systems didn't want bandits to be able to take out freighters from a mountain top.

Sloane tried to throw up her hands, but the cuffs caught

her wrists, tugging them back toward the sheets. "You're incredibly naive for a military man, Fortune."

Gareth frowned. "There's a hand cannon on this ship, isn't there?"

Sloane folded her arms across her chest, tilting her chin in the air. "I prefer not to answer that."

Gareth stood. "I should let you rest."

"Yeah, you should. Bye now."

As Gareth slipped out of the room, though, he had the distinct impression that she was smiling.

CHAPTER 13

WHEN SLOANE GOT TOO restless to stay in the infirmary —which happened very shortly after Fortune's visit but was not in any way related—she busted out of her nursing cuffs, ignoring the way they scolded her. Her head was only throbbing lightly, and her neck was hardly sore, so she snagged the ship's manual out of her cabin before thumping her way down to cargo to spend some time reading it.

And in cargo she'd stayed, sitting cross-legged against the sealed gangplank with the manual spread across her lap. With Brighton in the crate to her right and Bellow still chilling on the left, she felt like a jailer.

"Okay," she said, "why would someone leave a note in the margin suggesting three keys on the main engine compartment rather than four? More is better, right?"

"You probably shouldn't be asking your prisoners for assistance with your engine." Bellow's voice was a half-whine, half-growl, like a wolf having a bad day. Or a puppy, practicing ways to sound tough. He was lying on the floor in the middle of his crate-cell, his figure just a lump of a shadow.

Sloane had to refrain from throwing the book at his crate. She'd only have to go pick it up. "I wasn't asking you; I was asking Brighton."

She could see Brighton more clearly, as he was leaning against the side of the crate and peering out at her. He had to stoop, just slightly, to keep from bumping his head on the ceiling. "He's not wrong, you know," he said. "About asking your prisoners for advice."

"But you know the answer."

"He should!" BRO chimed in. "His official record shows jobs as a ship's mechanic, information officer, mechanic again, bruiser—what's a bruiser?—and freelancer. What's a freelancer?"

"I gave you access to the public feeds for a reason," Sloane said. "Look it up."

BRO seemed to have no trouble looking up obscure knowledge about jungle planets or checking the thesaurus. But for some things, it appeared to need permission. Or, better programming. Maybe it was just making conversation. She couldn't tell.

At the moment, BRO was still marginally more helpful than it was annoying. As long as it stayed that way, she wouldn't complain. Much.

Brighton said, "Three keys is better because it's the minimum you can have for safety. Four's better, but three gets you in faster in a pinch. Some captains find themselves in a pinch more than others."

Sloane flipped the page. "Isn't that the truth? So, is it fair to assume that most of these margin notes are along the same lines?"

"Maybe. Hard to say without a good look around the engine."

Bellow snorted.

"Don't you have a nice, self-righteous Fleet Commander on your ship who could answer these questions for you?" Brighton asked. "I'd be willing to bet he'd help you out."

Bellow snorted again. "Oh, he'd help her. He'd help her right out of her—"

"Finish that sentence," Brighton interrupted, "and I'll bust out of here so I can shut you up myself."

"You're her prisoner, too," Bellow said sulkily.

Sloane shook her head. She didn't know why Brighton was defending her honor—it was shredded beyond repair, anyway, and sex had nothing to do with it—but it kept her from having to make the threats, so fine. "I like it down here," she said.

The prisoners might be annoying, but they didn't stare her down with their earnest gray eyes. Fakely earnest gray eyes, she reminded herself. There was nothing real about a man who acted like he was the supreme moral center of the galaxy while he secretly plotted to take it over. Or so Uncle Vin had believed.

Brighton drummed his fingers on the side of the crate, still staring at Bellow like he wanted to storm over there and rip the guy's throat out. Did those two have a history or something? He couldn't really be that upset at the suggestion that Fortune liked her. First, it was a ridiculous notion —she didn't think that man liked anyone who wasn't swathed in Fleet blue—and second, who cared?

"She's avoiding Commander Fortune!" BRO said.

Sloane frowned. "I am not."

"Yes, you are. You waited an extra seven-point-five seconds to exit your room because I told you he was passing in the hall. You said, and I quote, 'Doesn't he ever sleep?' And then you made me tell you when, and I quote, the 'Coast was clear.'"

Sloane wished BRO had a physical body so she could kick it in the shins. "I just wanted to avoid a lecture on leaving the infirmary early."

Bellow laughed like he didn't quite believe that, but she didn't care. It was true enough. She hadn't expected Fortune to visit her in the infirmary—she'd barely remembered he was on the ship at all until he'd shown up there, looking all worried and smelling like soap.

She didn't know why she was disappointed that he hadn't owned up to the Olton Moon thing. She couldn't expect him to let her in on classified information, but something about the lie caught in her gut.

Which was rich, when she thought about it, since she was perfectly happy allowing him to believe she'd picked up a Federation-approved bounty on Cal Cornum. She hadn't *said* that Bellow was Federation-approved, but he'd assumed, and it was still a lie of omission.

At least she still had Brighton, and she *did* need to bring *him* to the Federation. So technically, it wasn't a lie at all.

Sloane snapped the book shut and pushed herself up to her feet. Her head was throbbing again, and she was aching for something to drink. "Call me if they try to kill each other, BRO," she said. "They're both worth money."

"Okay!"

Unfortunately, the kitchen was already occupied. Fortune was there, looking confused as he prodded at one of the acquisitions she'd made on her jaunt out of the galaxy. Her best acquisition, actually, and she was going to force Alex to risk the galaxy by opening a new wormhole when they ran out of fuel for it.

Sloane hesitated in the doorway, but BRO's nonsense about avoiding the Commander, and Bellow's laughter, were still ringing in her head. So she put on her best, most businesslike walk, and joined him at the counter.

"Feeling better?" he asked. He still smelled like soap, and his hair had dried now, enough that she could see the light streaks of gray running through the sides. It looked good on him.

Oh, Bellow would laugh even more at that. He really would.

She shrugged. "Well enough."

Fortune pointed at the gadget. "What is this thing?"

"This," she said, "is a beautiful, beautiful invention." She stuck a mug under the nozzle, pressed the button, and watched as a stream of dark liquid poured into the cup. It smelled like the best thing in the universe.

She added some milk, which she kept on hand for this purpose alone, and handed the cup to him. "Coffee."

He raised an eyebrow, then lifted the mug to his lips. "Good," he said.

"Not good. Fantastic. It's a stim drink."

He hesitated, eyes dropping to the cup, but she took the mug from him and swallowed a long sip. "Do not pretend you've never taken a stim before a mission," she said. "This is way better than some tasteless gel. Look, it's fine. Nothing too strong. Avoid it near bedtime, though. Ask me how I know."

He examined the cup for another moment, then turned back to the gadget to repeat her steps and make his own. "I've never heard of coffee."

The question was implied. It was a big galaxy, but Fortune had probably been to every inhabited System in it, or near enough. She was willing to bet, though, that he'd never been *outside* of it.

"Yeah," she said, "I picked it up in another galaxy. No big deal."

The moment the words had left her mouth, she wished she could snatch them back. What would she say, if he asked her to explain? She couldn't tell him about Alex's wormholes, and she didn't *want* to tell him the rest. Not when it started with Oliver and his betrayal. Not when it both started and ended with the biggest mistakes of Sloane's life, up until this point at least. Not that her mistakes would be likely to surprise him. Though their magnitude might give him pause.

He waited a moment, as if hoping she'd volunteer the story. When she didn't, though, he simply said, "If anyone could manage that, Ms. Tarnish, it would be you."

From someone else, it might have sounded like mocking. But she had the strangest feeling that he meant it.

When he finished making his own cup and turned back, he looked almost... relaxed. She hadn't thought any Fleet officer could look relaxed—their faces were like stone, most of the time—but the man was very nearly smiling. Miracle of miracles. "How's it made?" he asked.

"From beans or something? I don't know. We'll run out eventually, so do not waste it or I'll kill you."

"I believe you."

The ship gave a slight lurch, followed by a dip—a sign that they were leaving the Current—and Sloane placed a hand on the counter to steady herself. Brighton's bounty posting had indicated that the Federation kept their headquarters at the outskirts of the Pike System, which meant *Moneymaker* would probably be able to land sooner than later.

Fortune was still looking down at her, like he had something more to say—hopefully about the coffee and not the galaxy it'd come from—when a red light flashed on above both doors. Followed by a ringing alarm, which cut off almost as soon as it began so that Hilda's voice could filter through a speaker in the ceiling. "Our dragon-winged friends are back," she said.

Fox Clan had followed them all the way out here? Those guys could really hold a grudge. "Dragon wings?" Sloane said. "I thought they looked like birds."

"They can be mosquitos for all I care. They're back. Flight deck. Now."

Sloane sighed. Sometimes it felt like she wasn't the captain here at all. She set her coffee lovingly in the sink as the attack alarms started to blare in earnest. Excellent.

"Who's attacking?" Fortune asked. "Who's got ships with wings?"

Sloane grabbed his arm and dragged him toward the flight deck. He might be useful there. "It's Fox Clan," she said. "They want Brighton."

CHAPTER 14

"BRIGHTON'S STILL ON YOUR *SHIP*?"

Sloane didn't know how Fortune managed to make himself heard over the commotion of *Moneymaker*'s alarms, but his voice was strong and clear, and full of consternation. So much for that smile.

She supposed it was part of being a Commander, yelling over alarms and such, but he didn't give any orders on this ship. If he didn't know that already, he'd learn it soon enough.

Her head only throbbed a little as she raced through the kitchen and through the storage bay to get to *Moneymaker*'s flight deck. For a midsized ship, it certainly had a grating scream. Lights flashed from the ceilings, and it was almost like the ship wanted to remind her that it'd *just* been fixed and could she *please* refrain from punching any more holes in its sides.

"I don't know why you're surprised," she shouted back at Fortune. "My ship couldn't leave the Bone System, remember?"

"Is he restrained?"

"Fortune, the guy is basically harmless. He's a hacker."

A hacker with big muscles, and mechanical skills, but still. Sloane had a feeling he was more teddy bear than killer. So he'd caused a few little computer issues. For the Fleet, probably, since they seemed to want him so badly—and for Fox Clan, too. He didn't pick his targets well, but otherwise he was fine. He'd defended her with Bellow, hadn't he? Unnecessarily, but still.

Also, and she definitely didn't want to bring this up since Fortune still thought that Bellow was also a Federation-approved bounty, but Fox Clan could definitely be after *her* now, too. Since she'd stolen the bounty posting out of their database. By accident, but she doubted they'd care about that.

Lastly, and perhaps most importantly, Brighton was locked in a wooden crate. She didn't think that was hackable.

Using the walls for support, Sloane threw herself into the flight deck and stumbled into the co-pilot's seat. "Can you silence those alarms?" Sloane asked.

Hilda punched a button, and the screeching stopped.

"Thank goodness!" BRO said. "My throat was getting sore!"

Fortune cast his gaze toward the ceiling. "Please tell me your onboard AI isn't accessible to Brighton."

"Of course it isn't." Sloane decided not to ask him to define 'accessible'—she was pretty sure the two had been playing word games the entire time she'd been on Cal Cornum—because now wasn't the time, and it wasn't any of his business, anyway.

Outside the viewport, a mottled planet grew larger by the minute, its surface marbled in yellow and blue. The blues were so dark they looked almost reflective, the yellows near to neon. Were those the *clouds*?

On Hilda's helpful dash screen, the Fox Clan ships had arranged themselves behind *Moneymaker* in a tight half-circle. The lines on the screen indicated that they were just outside of shooting range, and that Hilda was gunning it toward the Federation's home planet as fast as she could. Outrunning the Clanners was *Moneymaker*'s best bet, and the only way to avoid the fight altogether.

"What does the Federation call their HQ?" Sloane asked. "I feel like I should know that."

"The Federation." Fortune was holding onto the door-frame like he might bolt out of the room at any second. Where he thought he'd go, she didn't know.

Sloane frowned. "Just 'the Federation'? What's their address, The Federation at One Federation Way, Federation Planet, Pike System?"

The corner of Fortune's lip quirked. "Probably."

The man could understand a joke. Remarkable.

Hilda's dashboard screen beeped as the Fox Clan ships picked up speed, moving together in synch, and Sloane tried to remember what Uncle Vin had told her about the thieves. They liked weaponized body mods—unpleasant to install—and they disliked AI assistants.

She could most likely use that if she had to.

So far, it didn't seem necessary. The *Moneymaker* dot on the screen kept just out of shooting range, and Hilda caressed the dash with a loving pat. "Moving fast again," she said. "Not as fast as she *could*, but she's overcoming that limp. Thanks, Commander."

Fortune strapped himself into the jump-seat behind Sloane's chair and leaned forward until the straps strained. "Tell me," he said. "Does your father know where you are?"

"That's what my high school boyfriend used to say," Hilda said.

Of all the times for her father to come up, honestly. How long had Fortune been wanting to ask her that? Sloane hadn't talked to her father since she'd crossed the wrong criminals—the wrongest of all criminals—during that jaunt to the Milky Way. She'd gotten him held as a hostage, but he was safe, now, along with her mother and little sister. That was all she knew.

"Why?" Sloane asked. "You know my father?"

"Everyone knows Zander, Ms. Tarnish," Fortune said.

"It's part of what makes Sloane so mysterious," Hilda added.

Yeah. She was aware. She twisted around to look the Commander in the eye. "But you talk about him like you really know him. Did you go to school with him or something?"

Fortune blinked, opened his mouth, then closed it. "The man's three decades older than I am. Easily."

Sloane put on her best frown. "Be fair, Fortune. He's not eighty yet."

Fortune just stared at her. She liked it when he stared. It seemed like a pretty clear indication that she'd managed to stump him into silence. "You think I'm fifty?"

Hilda sighed. "And I owe you that drink."

Sloane had to suppress a grin. "A Center System drink, remember. That's gonna cost you."

Sloane watched Fortune's gaze slip back and forth between them, like he wasn't sure what to think, or what to do. It was cute, in a way. "You bet on my age."

"Well, *first* we bet on your age," Hilda said, "but then Sloane wanted to bet you'd be upset if she said she thought you were fifty. You shouldn't be upset, Commander. *I'm fifty*."

"I'm not ups... We're being *attacked* right now."

"Don't change the subject," Hilda said. "Technically they're too far to attack."

"He's got a point," Sloane said. "Work first, then play. They're gaining."

Fortune's mechanic might've given *Moneymaker* her speed back, but the Fox Clan semicircle was still cruising toward them at a neat clip. The Federation swelled in the viewport—it was such a power move, to name the entire planet after themselves—but not quickly enough. They were probably going to need to start stalling soon.

Time for some innovative thinking.

"Right," Sloane said, "do you still have that stun cable, Fortune?"

There was a brief pause. "Yes." The word was drawn out, like he would have rather kept it in his mouth.

"Trying not to take it personally that you never want to share your weapons with me," Sloane said. "Now listen, I'm thinking we find a way to shoot the cables out, short their drives, and get away. The end."

Fortune leaned forward, touching his fingertips to the arm of her chair. "Those cables are for capturing *people*. We use a similar device for disabling the ships, and it easily uses a hundred times more power."

"What a waste," Sloane said, "because this will work."

"I can assure you that it won't."

Sloane looked out at the ships. They were so hulky, and they looked so... catchable, with all those wing parts. "OK. Then we use the cable to lasso them."

"The cables won't hold." He was still leaning forward,

still in her space. It was annoying. "Why don't you just shoot at them?"

Sloane hitched a thumb back over her shoulder to point at him and narrowly missed poking him in the face. He was leaning in closer than she'd thought. "Because you didn't have our ammo refilled."

"Truth," Hilda said.

The Fleet Commander could pretend he didn't know anything about the base on Olton Moon as long as he wanted, but there was definitely a reason he hadn't had his mechanic refill *Moneymaker*'s plasma reserves. So no, Sloane didn't trust the Commander of the Galactic Fleet, no matter how flummoxed he looked, no matter how gray his eyes were. She didn't trust him for a second.

Fortune sat back in his chair, pressing a fingertip to his temple. "How is this *my* fault?"

"You'll have to get them to unfurl those wings if you want to catch them with a cable," Hilda said, ignoring his comment.

Sloane shot the pilot a grateful look. Hilda nodded back.

"Why are you *listening* to this plan?" Fortune asked.

"Because this woman is never wrong," Hilda snapped back. It was absolutely, unequivocally wrong—Sloane had nearly ended the universe once; good times—but Hilda's support made her chest expand with something hot and almost tearful. Almost. "Her schemes sound like madness, but they work. So shut up and let her do her thing."

To Sloane's surprise, Fortune actually did shut up.

"OK," Sloane said, "we close in on Federation. We descend into atmo, we loose the cables, and—"

"Lager," Fortune said, and Sloane thought the man was ordering a beer until she turned to see the Commander with his fliptab open in his palm. A little, blue-lined officer stood in his hand. "Disable the Fox Clan ships, will you?"

The holo-officer nodded. Before Sloane could ask what the hell was happening, a Fleet frigate materialized directly outside the viewport and off to the left. Not at some distance behind *Moneymaker*, not soaring in from the Current because it'd just happened to be passing nearby, but *right there*. The ship had been *right there*, close enough to spit at, and Sloane hadn't seen it. The instruments hadn't picked up on it, either.

But how? She didn't know of any tech that could do that. If the Fleet was using something like that, people would've been talking about it. They weren't, which meant no one knew.

The Fleet could be hiding bases all over the galaxy, and no one would have any idea.

Uncle Vin was right. The Fleet had far too much power, and too many secrets.

In the end, the frigate didn't have to shoot. The Fox Clan ships took one look at it and spun back toward the Current.

"See?" Fortune said. "No harebrained schemes necessary. Just good, old-fashioned—"

"Show of force," Sloane interrupted. "A good, old-fashioned bully move."

Fortune took a long breath in, then let it out. "You wanted to lasso them and swing them back out into space. Which, by the way, wouldn't have worked, because the cables would have snapped. But if it *had*, you could have fried all their systems in the process, including life support. How's that better?"

It wasn't. Not really. But Sloane couldn't help the spark of indignation that was burning up her throat and getting hotter with every word that came out of his mouth. She *should* be upset because he hadn't flexed his ugly ship at the Fox Clan ships sooner, and because he'd had his big-brother frigate secretly babysitting her like she was a misbehaving toddler.

But no, she was *actually* upset because he hadn't trusted her to carry out a solid plan, to escape by her own wits.

It was ridiculous, and it made no sense, but she didn't care.

Before she could work out the best way to yell at him about it, Alex appeared from belowdecks, her red hair pulled back in a messy bun. She had a streak of grease on her face and spots of red flushing her cheeks.

"We've got bigger problems than whatever you're fighting about," she said. "I don't know what kind of cheap glue your mechanic friend used on the engine, but it's coming loose. The whole thing's about to overheat."

Sloane cursed, unlatched her belt, and dove after Alex. "I'll deal with you later," she said, stabbing Fortune in the chest with her finger as she passed. "Don't follow me."

CHAPTER 15

GARETH WOULDN'T HAVE BEEN ALL that surprised if Sloane Tarnish knew exactly how to keep a star schooner's engine from overheating. He honestly wouldn't have been all that surprised if she'd enacted her ship-grabbing cable scheme and somehow, through grace or luck or sheer nerve, managed to bend the laws of physics to her will to *make* it work.

But he'd spent most of his life on one ship or another, and every Fleet officer spent at least one rotation assisting the mechanics and engineers. When disaster struck, you needed knowledgeable hands to help.

So, despite her command—the woman could've been a commander herself—Gareth unstrapped himself from the chair and went after her. If nothing else, he could lend a hand.

The ship pitched to the side, and Gareth grabbed a storage shelf to keep his balance as his feet left the floor for an instant longer than they should have. The gravity anchors were fritzing, definitely a sign of overheating systems.

Sloane barely seemed to notice. She was already hurrying through the kitchen. Every time the ship lurched, she hit a counter or booth and pushed off as hard as she could, giving herself an extra boost in the waning gravity.

He caught up with her in the infirmary, sticking to her heels as she pushed straight through to the tail of the ship. Engineering bay, in every schooner he'd ever seen. She'd swiped a thick book from the floor of the kitchen on her way back, and though he couldn't see the cover, he knew of only one kind of analogue book that was guaranteed to be on almost every ship in the galaxy. The woman was bringing the ship's manual back to the engine room with her.

"I thought you said you were studying medicine," he said, "not engineering."

She slammed her palm to the side of the door—she had basic security, that was good—and pushed inside. He half expected her to lock him out, but she didn't. "I was," she said, "but the engine won't fix itself. So here we are."

The bay was too hot, the air thick with melted plastic and overheated metal. No smoke, not yet, but he could almost feel a fire about to burst into the space at any second. Which would eat the schooner's oxygen supply in minutes, not to mention compromising the integrity of its hull.

He had a feeling Sloane wouldn't appreciate it if she pointed that out.

Gareth sent a silent message to Lager, asking him to stay close. *Might need an evac.*

On it, sir.

Gareth rolled his sleeves to the elbows, glancing around. "Where's your equipment case?"

They'd need protective gloves, and probably a few new lines of cable. He'd smelled that rancid-plastic odor before, and it usually meant melted casings.

When Sloane didn't answer, he looked at her. She was just staring at him, her lips pressed thin, and the look in her eyes sparked hot with anger. Hotter than the room. Sweat was beading on her forehead, and she was staring at him like it was his fault.

"What?" he said.

She pointed a finger at him. "I don't trust you. You follow me with secret stealth ships, you hold back on helping in the fight, and you undermine my plans."

He honestly couldn't tell which accusation was making her angriest. As for Fleet secrets, she ought to know they had some; they couldn't well let all the criminals in the galaxy know what they were capable of at every turn. Gareth had a dozen such secrets brewing in labs throughout Cadence. It was a necessity.

He had a feeling, though, that she was mostly upset about his objection to her ship-lassoing plan. Which sounded good in theory but would not have worked. It simply wouldn't have.

Gareth glanced around, found a large box attached to the wall, and touched the latch carefully. It was still cool, or at least touchable. Sloane's uncle kept good equipment on his ship. He opened the door, slid on a pair of gloves, and started picking tools out of the cabinet. A wrench, a line of cable, and some patching plaster would work.

When he turned away from the box, Sloane was blocking his path to the engine. What did she think he was going to do, blow up their ship? If he wanted to do that, he'd just let the engine overheat. She was dangerously close to allowing that to happen, anyway.

He sighed. "The cables would never have held one of those ships," he said, "and you had six of them on your tail. Your stunts are smart, Ms. Tarnish, I grant you, but—"

"*Stunts?*" He expression was all outrage, which was ironic since he should be the one railing at her for interrupting his attempt to save all their lives.

"Yes, stunts." He couldn't keep the heat out of his voice. He didn't try. Sometimes, patience could kill. "You're smart, and you're innovative, but you always look for the easy way out. Every time. And it's going to get you killed."

Her hands were shaking, her cheeks flushing red. It might've been the temperature, but he thought it was anger. "I look for solutions no one else sees. Because everyone else's heads are stuck so deep into their rule books that they can't see their cannons are wide enough to crawl through."

"And I suppose you're planning to use that same thinking on the engine? What's your plan, to thump the thing extra hard until it works?"

Sloane sniffed, hugging the manual to her chest. The thing was bursting with extra scraps of paper. Had she been studying it? She'd carried it into the kitchen with her, hadn't she? "I could do without the condescension," she said. "And no. I was going to reboot it."

Gareth took a deep breath in—there was a thread of smoke now, he could smell it—and handed her a tube of patching plaster. "You can't con an engine into working right," he said. "Let me help you."

For a second, he thought she was going to refuse. He'd have to call Lager and force her off the ship before it exploded, and then she'd hate him even more. He didn't know why the idea of her hatred caught in the back of his throat the way it did.

But Sloane glanced at the choking engine, then back at him, and she gave him a tight nod.

It only took half an hour to get the engine emergency under control. But this ship needed to be Current worthy if he was going to get it to a more trustworthy mechanic after their meeting with the Federation—he'd be having a stern conversation with his contact back in Adu—so they stayed for another hour, patching cracks and tightening bolts, and generally putting the place back together.

Sloane must have been doing well in her medical studies, before her uncle had disappeared. She was a quick study, and once she decided to listen, she did it. She asked smart questions, and yes, she saw solutions he would have overlooked. Not a stun cable roping a three-ton ship, maybe, but a dab of plaster to a split cable rather than replacing the whole line, or a quick solder that would hold longer than a patch job.

Gareth found himself wondering what area of medicine she'd been specializing in, back at the Academy. He'd been surprised when Zander had said she was studying medicine; Gareth would have expected something to do with art. At least, when he'd met her for the first time, at the Fleet ball on Anro Moon, she'd looked at the sculptures in the garden with true appreciation. And she'd certainly demonstrated her knowledge about them.

He wouldn't recommend pushing the ship to its max speed, not quite yet. But it would do for now.

When they were done, Gareth's neck was sore from bending over engine parts, but the temperature had dropped to normal levels, and he no longer had to anchor himself to make sure his feet stayed on the ground.

Sloane placed her tools carefully back in the case on the wall, settling each into its proper place. He'd half expected her to throw them in. "I want a Center System mechanic when you fix my ship again," she said. "Or you could do it yourself, piece by piece. Whichever is more expensive, since it's on your tab."

Gareth wiped his hands on a cloth and hung it back on the wall. "My fixes are bandages, at best."

Sloane shrugged, but she was smiling. She wasn't angry at him anymore. At least, not for now. She started to move past him, but something made him touch a hand to her shoulder. She stopped, and he tried not to see the suspicion that immediately darkened her eyes.

"For the record," he said, "if you were a Fleet soldier, I'd have promoted you up the ranks as quickly as possible out of respect for your sheer innovation. And boldness."

She pointed the empty tube of glue at him, then tossed it into the recycler by her feet. "Don't try to recruit me, Fortune. I'd never enlist, and you can't afford me, anyway. Now let's go tell Hilda it's time to land."

CHAPTER 16

MONEYMAKER HAD BEEN CLEARED to land in a pristine spaceport with walls so smooth they might've been made of polished rock. The whole place was as beautiful and streamlined as the greatest Center System cities. Pike was a Middle System, but was clearly looking to make a name for itself.

Sloane didn't know if the Federation's city was also called Federation, or if they'd branched out in this case. Whatever they called it, the city might have been Shard's polar opposite. Sparkling towers jutted up out of the same polished-stone pavement that defined the port, soaring toward the sky as if they hoped to one day scrape their way into the atmosphere. If there were any optimistic towers in the galaxy, these were them; they didn't share the monochrome darkness of the streets, instead gleaming in various shades the rainbow. With a definite preference for silver, blue, and gold.

It might've been overwhelming. Instead, it was alluring. Like a dream. Like a promise.

With every step she took, blinking signs advertised

theater shows and high-end shops, and the whole street simmered with the smell of butter and garlic and herbs. When was the last time she'd eaten in a restaurant? Any restaurant? Oliver certainly hadn't taken her to any.

The streets here weren't overly crowded, and none of the people looked hurried as they strolled along. They tended to wear bright colors, as if in homage to their rainbow of towers, though in a city like this one, surely some of them had to be tourists. In long pants, short, belted tunics, and vests, they walked in pairs and trios, stepped in and out of exterior elevators, and generally seemed to be having a good time.

This city was alive with possibilities.

There were even galleries, dozens of them, their windows wide and welcoming, with a variety of artwork spotlighted in each display. She tried not to slow, to peer at brushstrokes and attempt to identify their artists before reading the placards—she probably couldn't, but it was a good game—though it wasn't easy to keep up her pace. She wanted nothing more than to lose herself in a room full of sculptures for an hour.

But she could tell from the way that Fortune strode by her side, tense and watchful, that he was in the all-business mode. She doubted he'd be willing to entertain any distractions from the mission. The Commander had helped her fix *Moneymaker*, it was true, but she'd do well to remember that he had his own agenda here.

A hov-train wove through the skyscrapers above their heads and huffed to a stop about midway up the closest tower, where a balcony extended from the building like a narrow tongue, giving passengers a place to disembark. Sloane couldn't see to the tops of the towers, not quite, but there was probably another hov-train that circled above them.

"I bet these hov-trains don't connect to any gravity anchors," Sloane said.

Fortune cast a glance along the street, as if looking for the telltale silver-coin look of the anchors. Sloane didn't see any, either; Federation probably had its own gravity.

"If they did before, they definitely don't now," he said dryly. He seemed to be on the edge of a smile. Yeah, that'd been a good stunt. The fact that he thought so, too, even though she'd beaten *him* during it... But no. She couldn't let herself think of him like a friend.

She'd been doing her best to stay angry since the incident with the Fox Clan ships, but it wasn't as easy as she'd anticipated. He'd helped her fix *Moneymaker*, and he hadn't even been condescending about it. Since then, they seemed to have settled into an uneasy, albeit unspoken, truce. She hadn't brought up any more accusations, and he hadn't criticized her for being herself.

She couldn't let herself forget that this man had a suite of hidden technology at his fingertips, that he could hide entire frigates with a snap of his fingers and a tap of his fliptab. He also insisted on denying that his ships were jockeying for space in the Bone System along with every criminal in the galaxy. She knew what she'd seen. She knew it was a lie.

And more likely than not, Fortune had something to do with Uncle Vin's disappearance. Vin had disappeared a full year after Sloane had lifted Fleet intelligence for him—intelligence that he'd claimed would prove their intention to take over the galaxy. Time had made it seem unlikely that the data and the disappearance were related. But what if they were?

She couldn't trust the Commander. And she absolutely refused to *like* him.

"Do you know where we're headed?" Fortune asked.

She didn't. But the Federation already knew they were there—they'd been the ones to clear *Moneymaker*'s landing —and she had a feeling they'd be the ones to come to her.

Before she could say as much, a man in a sleeveless purple tunic separated himself from a nearby crowd and approached them with a bow. He had bright blue hair that matched his belt, and yellow shoes. The whole ensemble made Sloane want to squint.

"Ms. Tarnish," the man said, ignoring Fortune completely as he offered her a short bow. There were deep lines around his mouth, though he otherwise looked rather young. "Welcome to Federation."

It was almost like he'd been listening to them, waiting for one of them to mention the Federation. In fact, Fortune was glancing around as if searching for hidden mics. He shouldn't bother. If Sloane had designed this place, she'd have made the whole street into a mic. Why not?

"I'm Ambassador Freic, of the Cosmic Trade Federation," the man continued. "With your permission, we'll check on your bounty."

"Go ahead," Sloane said. "He's on the ship. My pilot will let you in."

Probably. Sloane sent a silent note to Hilda, just in case.

"Bounties," Fortune said. Sloane and Freic both turned to look at him when he spoke. "There are two. Yes?"

The ambassador looked at Fortune, then at Sloane. "Follow me," he said. "The Coordinator wants to meet you."

He started down the street, inviting her to join him with a gesture. Sloane fell into step beside him.

"I guess I'll just tag along then," Fortune muttered.

Sloane hadn't allowed him access to her silent messaging, and she didn't intend to. But if she *did*, she'd have told him that there were places in the galaxy that didn't bend knee to the Fleet and weren't impressed by his title. And she hoped it would stay that way.

It was refreshing, in a way, to land in a place that ignored Fleet titles.

"How old is Federation City?" Sloane asked, more to make conversation than because she wanted to know.

Freic chuckled. "It's Obsidian City, though I see why you'd make that assumption. The CTF has been headquartered here for almost a century—we'll be celebrating our centennial in three years, in fact—but the city is much older than that."

Sloane reached back into her grade school lessons, trying to recall what she'd learned about the CTF. Not a lot. "The Fleet's what, a little over a hundred years old?"

"A hundred and nine," Fortune said.

"Thank you, Fortune, very helpful," she said. "I didn't know they'd been founded so close together."

Freic gave her a secret kind of smile, one that should have accompanied a wink. "Some would say that one necessitated the other."

Was he implying that the Federation had been founded as a reaction to the Fleet's founding? That was interesting. They did such different things, though clearly their paths crossed occasionally. But then, one source of power in the galaxy should have a counterbalance. It made some sense.

Fortune didn't respond. She didn't turn to look at him, but she suspected that if she did, she'd find him wearing that inscrutable mask he loved so much. The man wore that straight-faced look like armor.

Ambassador Freic led them through a passage where the ubiquitous black stone of this city had been sculpted into a sweeping arch of charred pearls. When they reached the other side, a large courtyard opened up, with a fountain in the center and a triple layer of arched windows that looked out from three of the enclosing walls. It reminded Sloane of the fighting ring on Shard, a bit, except that these buildings were all made of that same black polished stone.

There were people on the balconies, and people in the square, their tunics and robes and slacks—and hair, and jewelry—just as brightly colored as those she'd seen in the street. Every single one had their attention directed to the screen that took up the entire wall of the fourth building.

No archways there. Just numbers. And whenever they flickered or changed, the people started shouting and pointing at each other, or staring off into space like they were making silent calls on their eye screens.

"This is the Trade Hub," Freic said. "The CTF conducts the majority of its business right here."

Sloane had known that bounty regulation was a crumb of the larger organization. But to see the Federation's business in action, those number spiraling across the screen... She had a feeling she'd still been underestimating them.

She paused, taking a moment to glance back at Fortune. He was just standing there, hands at his sides. He didn't look surprised at all.

Freic let Sloane admire the square for a few beats before bowing her into a passage that ran beneath the closest building. She had the distinct impression that he'd walked her through the square on purpose—only she couldn't imagine why. Did he want her to be impressed?

The ambassador ushered her into a hallway that seemed to be caught halfway between beauty and function. There weren't any fancy chandeliers or billion-token sculptures around, but the whole place also glittered like it hadn't ever seen a speck of dust.

Freic brought them to the first door, opened it, and bowed them in. "Good luck," he said.

All right, then. Sloane nodded and slipped into the room.

The man she'd seen briefly in holograph form sat on a desk in the center of the room with one leg touching the floor and the other bent sideways as he watched a flicker of numbers pass by on his wall-sized screen. The same ones, Sloane would have wagered, as the ones that streamed across the square outside.

"I usually don't meet hunters myself." The man didn't look away from the screen. He might've been talking to himself. "But I've heard so much about you, I couldn't resist."

In her ear, BRO—who'd been mercifully silent up until this point—said, "And he talked to you, too! When we called him!"

Let's not remind him, she sent.

The Coordinator turned away from the screen, remaining seated on his desk. He had one arm crossed over his chest, the other hand lifted as though to prop up his chin —or possibly to display the rings that glinted on his fingers, each set with gold, diamond, jaevin, and other precious materials. Some of the rings extended all the way to his first knuckle. His hair was flame red, and he wore the same vest she'd seen him in on the holo.

"I didn't expect you to bring a friend, however," he said. "Commander?"

Sloane hadn't been invited to sit, but she decided to do it anyway, dropping into one of the black-stone chairs clustered in the center of the room. It was easily the most uncomfortable seat she'd ever taken. "He's not my friend. We cut a deal."

The Coordinator showed his teeth, a wolfish sort of a smile. "Did you, now? I'm intrigued." He dropped his hands, leaning them on his thighs, and studied Fortune with open interest. Sloane decided he was handsome, in an offbeat, dangerous kind of way. Her type, then. Best to steer clear.

"Actually, I'm glad you're here, Gareth," the Coordinator said. "I've got a question for you."

Gareth. She supposed she must have known Fortune's first name—the man's face was splashed across the news feeds often enough that there must have been a name to accompany it at least sometimes—but it sounded wrong coming out of the Coordinator's mouth.

If Fortune thought so, he didn't let on. He did twitch an eyebrow, but Sloane was pretty sure it was a calculated one. "Oh?"

The Coordinator waited, and the two men stared each other down. They might've been opposing bookends—one dark and upright, the other unpredictable and wild. Both dangerous men, really.

"Get on with it, then, Striker," Fortune said. "I haven't got all day."

Of course Fortune knew the Coordinator's name. What kind of game had she stumbled into here?

The way they were staring at each other suggested it wasn't a game at all though.

Striker smiled, and this time it almost looked genuine. "I've been wondering, Commander. Why is the Fleet willing to allow a bounty capture that wasn't Federation approved? And right under your nose, no less?"

Sloane's mouth went dry, and she swallowed. She hadn't expected that little detail to come up so soon.

Fortune's gaze slid to hers and held. She didn't look away; she owed him that much. Whatever he saw in her expression, it must have confirmed the Coordinator's accusations, because he gave his head a minuscule shake, and she thought—she might have imagined it, but she thought she heard him sigh.

Heat rose into her cheeks, but she couldn't feel bad about the deception. She might not have chosen this path for herself, but she was what she was: a mercenary, a thief, and a liar. He shouldn't expect more than that from her.

CHAPTER 17

GARETH HAD MADE AN ASSUMPTION. He saw that now, the reflection of his carelessness in Sloane's expression. The woman might've shown an ounce of shame for her deception, but she just looked back at him with that cool, wide-eyed stare. The same one she'd used on him when they'd met at that ball on Anro Moon.

The same one that kept *working*, while he kept trying to make excuses for her, to understand why she'd left her life on Elter to take up her criminal uncle's legacy. The woman certainly didn't shy away from muddy planets or complicated engine rooms—or unapproved bounty postings, apparently—yet she also didn't seem like she particularly wanted to do any of it. What was her goal?

Some part of him kept reaching for explanations—blackmail, threats, or dangerous debt—but looking into her face now, he wondered if it was just part of who she was.

With difficulty, Gareth forced his focus away from Sloane to settle his gaze on Striker. This might be his only chance to meet with the Coordinator. The Federation might've opened its doors to the *Moneymaker*, but this place was notoriously unwelcoming. Especially to the Fleet.

Ultimately, it didn't matter that Sloane had deceived him; she'd still held to their deal, and Gareth wouldn't be the one to blow it.

And yet instead of confronting the Coordinator with the larger issue at hand, Gareth found himself stuck on the subject of the unapproved bounty. "Osmond Clay asked me to retrieve Jackson Bellow," he said. "Are you saying he tried to get around the Federation, too?"

Striker waved a hand, his rings ticking with the flutter of his fingers. "Of course. We'd never have allowed an assassination attempt."

Wouldn't they, though? Gareth wasn't so sure.

"You really should look into these things ahead of time, Fortune," Sloane said. She still looked like she didn't care, but there was a raw edge to her voice that he hadn't heard before. Perhaps she did know she shouldn't have lied.

And she wasn't wrong, either. Clay might've sent the Fleet on his little errand without Federation approval—the Fleet hardly needed to go begging to Striker to conduct their own operations—but Gareth should have at least confirmed that the job Sloane had taken was Federation approved.

How had she even *found* an unapproved job? And who had posted it?

"It is a problem, and one I hope we can discuss," Gareth said, "but it's not why I'm here."

To Gareth's surprise, Striker looked to Sloane. "I can escort the Commander back to his ship, if you like. It's lurking nearby, yes?"

Gareth managed to keep his jaw from falling open in surprise, but it was a narrow thing. How could Striker know about the frigate? *Sabre* was waiting outside of atmo, it was true, but unless something had gone wrong with the systems, the ship was back in stealth mode.

Maybe Striker's people had simply caught the battle with the Fox Clan. Maybe he was guessing.

Or maybe there was a mole in the Fleet.

"A deal's a deal," Sloane said. "Hear him out."

If Striker wanted to toss Gareth out on his ear, he could. Not physically, maybe—the man was a stick—but the whole planet was designed to answer to his will. These shiny obsidian walls listened to every word they said, and Gareth wouldn't have been surprised in the least if they were to grow spikes. Or perhaps shackles.

The Fleet wasn't the only organization that developed secret tech.

He didn't know how Sloane had ended up in this world, but she truly did navigate it as if it belonged to her. And when she spoke, the Coordinator nodded and looked to Gareth expectantly. If nothing else, the Federation could respect the terms of a deal.

What kind of a mess had he stepped into here? There was no telling, not with the information currently at his disposal.

But Gareth needed to keep Adu System safe, and to stop the chaos from spreading. That was the goal, the mission that mattered. He might not need the Federation's cooperation to do it, but he'd be a fool to think their assistance wouldn't help.

Striker spread his hands wide, as if in invitation. "All right, Commander. Enlighten us."

Oh, he intended to. He kept his place in the middle of the room, about halfway between the door and the seat Sloane had commandeered. His hands were relaxed at his sides; his expression was as neutral as he could make it.

That was key. "The Federation has been encroaching on Fleet territory, for one," he said. "And it's come to my attention that a CTF-approved bounty doesn't hold the same protections as it once did."

"Commander, be reasonable. Our interests are bound to cross from time to time."

Gareth waited a beat. When Striker didn't address the second complaint, he continued. "The Federation cannot send bounty hunters after Fleet-classed criminals. It's a clear violation of our operating agreement. I realize that our interests occasionally intersect, but we need to maintain separate areas of jurisdiction."

Striker slid down from the desk and brushed his hands together. The man looked like a walking matchstick, with his wiry muscles and that carrot-patch of hair. His energy felt coiled, too, as if there were hidden heat beneath every movement he made.

"Times have changed," Striker said. "That was a handshake agreement, made long ago. But it was also before the Fleet began taking steps to grab more of the Galaxy than you're meant to have."

At that, Sloane sat up in her chair, placing her feet flat on the floor. Gareth wanted to shake his head at her, to tell her to sit back, to hide her interest. Striker didn't need to know that she wanted more information about this particular accusation.

Gareth had heard it before, of course. The whispers ran that the Fleet had the strongest military in the Parse Galaxy, and that they could clench their fist around the free worlds in an instant.

These whisperers seemed to think the Fleet had several hundred more battleships than it actually did. These rumors tended to sprout up in systems that'd never needed the assistance of a few frigates to redirect an asteroid or discourage an incursion.

And they ignored the fact that the Fleet kept rigidly to its agreements. No boots on the ground except the three designated spots in Cadence, unless invited, and they answered to the Commission. *He* answered to the Commission.

If anyone affiliated with the Fleet wanted to establish an empire, Gareth had never met them. It didn't mean that person didn't exist, but he kept watch on every ship, every base, every asset. A former Fleet officer would have a tough time of it trying to steal or otherwise siphon Fleet resources away. A very tough time.

It was a big galaxy. Anyone hoping to establish an empire would need the kinds of resources that could never vanish without Gareth's knowledge. Not if they were supposedly disappearing from the Fleet's inventories.

And Striker had to know it. The man knew *Sabre* was stalking the space above his planet, so he had the means. If Gareth hadn't found anything that pointed to underhanded Fleet operations, then neither had Striker. But with Sloane sitting on the edge of her chair like that, the Coordinator knew he had a captive audience.

"And you have evidence of our supposed crimes?" Gareth asked.

Striker took a step toward him. "It's funny," he said. "But everyone who managed to capture any evidence has disappeared."

At that, Sloane drew in an audible hiss of breath. So, she did have a personal investment in this conversation.

And Striker had to know it. Gareth wished he had access to her direct comms, so he could send her a silent message, though he suspected Striker would see anything he wrote to her, anyway. The man was pretending to push Gareth's buttons, but he was actually working her. Why?

When Gareth had first met Sloane at the Fleet ball on Anro Moon, she'd been working with her uncle to steal a data key of intelligence out from under his nose. He never knew if she'd been the one to take it, but the key had never been recovered. He'd been forced to receive the reports directly from the spy, which wasn't the usual protocol.

The reports had nothing to do with galactic conspiracies or would-be empires. They'd merely been tracking Federation supply lines. Dry data, really. Gareth hadn't wanted to retrieve it personally at all, especially since it'd meant attending a ball, but it was protocol, and protocol mattered.

Vincent Tarnish had disappeared what, a year after that? Not quickly enough that Gareth had ever linked the two events. The man had no doubt angered any number of powerful people in the meantime. Could his disappearance be linked to that data key?

Striker was still watching him, standing almost too close, and much too still. Like a fox stalking its prey.

"What are you saying, Striker?" Gareth asked.

Striker leaned forward, crossing the invisible boundary into Gareth's personal space, and looked him directly in the eye. No, not a fox; the man was a viper. "I'd expect a man of your education to have pieced it together, Commander, but I'm suggesting that the Fleet made those people disappear."

Gareth didn't look at Sloane. He didn't want Striker to know that he understood the purpose of this conversation. As far as he knew, the man couldn't hack his thoughts. At least, not yet. "And in practical terms?"

"Ever the realist, eh Gareth?"

"First line in the job description."

Striker stared at him for a long moment, staying right

inside the line of Gareth's personal space. But Gareth had been threatened by more intimidating men than this CTF pretender, and he just stared Striker down until the man smiled—as if he'd won, somehow—and relaxed away. Like he'd just been passing through.

"In practical terms," Striker said, "it means that I no longer feel comfortable leaving *any* criminals to your... jurisdiction."

"And I'm meant to feel comfortable leaving them in yours?"

The Commission wasn't going to like that. They weren't going to like it at all. The Fleet and the Federation had a long history of tension, with their goals often at odds, but in the end both organizations worked together. They had to.

Striker stalked to the door and swung it open, even though he could have used a button for that. "I've nothing else to say to you, Commander. Will your frigate be sending a pod for you, or shall I arrange one?"

Gareth wished he'd brought Lager with him. Or an entire platoon. Though he had to concede that their presence wouldn't exactly have lent credence to the Fleet's innocence.

Now, though, he had no way to resist the clear dismissal without causing a major incident. And yet he hesitated, his gaze drifting over at Sloane before he could catch it.

"I'm fine." She looked toward him but avoided meeting his eyes. She wasn't buying into this story of Striker's, was she?

Or had she *already* suspected him of abducting her uncle, or of murdering him? For some reason, the thought sparked prickles of regret through his ribcage, and he felt his throat tighten. *She* didn't think he meant to take over the galaxy, did she? He searched her expression, looking for clues, but her eyes were shuttered now. Nothing to show.

"You should go." She pointed a shaky index finger in his direction, yet still managed to avoid meeting his gaze directly. "But you still owe me for ship repairs, don't forget."

Gareth wanted to stay, but he had to believe that Sloane could handle herself. This was her world, whether he liked it or not. And she wasn't his responsibility. Not that that little detail had ever stopped him from trying to save someone in the past. But what could he do? She was where she wanted to be, and he couldn't deny that the woman thrived here. If she learned to mask her reactions, she'd be unstoppable.

He headed for the door, pausing when he got to Striker. "I wouldn't step into a Federation-run pod if it was my only escape from a planet made of acid. Be careful here, Ms. Tarnish."

And with that, Gareth slipped out of the Coordinator's office and back into the city.

CHAPTER 18

SLOANE WATCHED as Fortune made his exit, somehow managing to look as if he were still in charge of the interaction, even though it'd been Striker who'd chased him out. She wasn't entirely sure she understood what history stood between these two—or if they were just jockeying on behalf of their organizations—but she did understand that Striker had information on Vin. Or at least, on the data Uncle Vin might have been chasing when he'd disappeared.

It was worth sticking around to find out.

Still, she couldn't help staring after Fortune even once the door closed. "Maybe I should follow him," she said. "Someone did just try to assassinate him."

With Fortune gone, the Coordinator's shoulders had relaxed, along with his smile. He made his way to the wall, touched a panel, and stepped back as a fully stocked bar glided out in front of him. "He'll get away safely, don't worry. His second-in-command sent guards to watch his back, and we allowed it. Not that he had any reason to fear in the first place. The Federation is a civilized place, Ms. Tarnish."

She adjusted in her seat. The rocky chair was uncomfortable against her legs, and her back was starting to ache. "If you're sure."

Striker poured a generous helping of clear liquid into two glasses, dropping a sprig of mint into each with a flourish. She'd have pictured him with one of those robotic bars, like the one her father had, but he obviously enjoyed concocting his own drinks. "You were right to bring the Cappel bounty to the Federation. We take unapproved postings very seriously."

"It was kind of an accident, if I'm being honest."

"A happy one, then." Striker handed her one of the glasses, and she waited for him to drink before taking a sip of her own. It tasted crisp and lightly citrusy, with a bite on the back of the tongue and a hint of that mint in the finish. Her father would have approved.

"Come," Striker said, "let me show you the Federation. The Fleet's had its time with you, and I should have my chance, too."

It was remarkable, really, how the man's body language had shifted. With Fortune in the room, Striker had been a wolf on the hunt, all tense muscles and toothy smiles. Now he was relaxed and easy. A little too charming, a little too smooth—Fortune had hardly needed to warn her, as if she had no common sense of her own—but clearly relieved at the Commander's absence.

Sloane dropped back the rest of her drink and stood. It was a relief to abandon the chair. "Let's do it."

Instead of taking her out the same way she'd entered, Striker ushered her through a second exit—the doors sealed so seamlessly into the wall that she'd never have noticed it—where the decor was much more elaborate than the original entrance hall. It was almost as if the Federation had two entrance halls, and they could choose which they decided to employ. Had the sparse corridor been for her benefit, or for Fortune's?

Here, paintings graced the walls at wide intervals, giving each canvas a wide margin to show off its brilliance. On the wall opposite to Striker's office, a canvas stretched to twice her height and three times as wide. It displayed an impossibly green scene, with hills and houses, a lake in the foreground, mountains in the distance. It was almost too beautiful, the light capturing the truth of a summer's day.

"I'm guessing you can name the painter." Striker paused beside her, folding his arms, his shoulder brushing against hers as he tilted his head to study the painting. He looked at it like he'd never seen it before.

Sloane could understand why. She couldn't look away from it herself. The hallway was wide enough to give her a good vantage, yet she found her feet were drifting closer. She wanted to drink in each cluster of animals, each suggestion of a forest. It was so realistic, as if riders might come bursting out from between the trees at any moment.

"I specialized in sculpture." She said it before she could stop herself, before she could consider that she was giving away valuable information about herself. Her voice sounded far away, as if it, too, were coming from the forest. A place for fairy tales.

Be careful here, Ms. Tarnish.

She'd try. Though maybe she'd do better to be careful with the Fleet. But anyway, what could Striker possibly do with information on her background in art?

"It's early Center System," she said. "They were obsessed with these pastoral pieces as they moved their terraforming efforts to the Middle Systems. They liked their idyllic nature scenes."

"Impressive."

She waved a hand in his direction without dropping her gaze from the painting, careful not to touch the canvas by accident. "Anyone who's watched a docu-vid on early Parse expansion could tell you as much."

"Oh, I doubt that. Do you have a guess, then? About the particular artist?"

Sloane leaned forward. The artist had used globs of paint, indicating a wealth of supply. Thin layers were common in the early Outer and Fringe movements, not that they'd have painted a pastoral scene like this. Anyone living there back then had been too busy trying to survive to spend much time on paintings. The brushstrokes here were so obvious that she could follow their pattern across the canvas. Almost as if she could imagine where the artist had begun, and where he'd ended up.

"Something in the Dhoman School, I think," she said.

"Dhoman himself, in fact. An original." He pointed at her, still smiling. "Not many people would know that."

Sloane couldn't help wishing that Uncle Vin had had time to teach her something about negotiation. It seemed like Striker was up to something—like he knew about her interest in art, and wanted to use it to distract her, or ingratiate himself. But what?

Sloane stepped away from the painting, and Striker started down the hall. There was a pearlescent archway at the far end, but paintings dotted the walls every few steps, and she could see a pair of sculptures waiting to be investigated. It was as if this hall had been designed specifically to hold her interest.

She could be suspicious. Or she could enjoy the fact that Striker was looking at each painting like he loved it as much as she did. She didn't meet many people who cared about art.

Just as she slowed to let her eyes drift along another painting, Striker spoke again. "What is it you want, Ms. Tarnish?" he asked.

That was easy. "I want the bounty money for Brighton."

He chuckled, pausing by a sculpture that was definitely a Vierni, with all that yellow-tinged brass. Striker ran a finger along the base, and she wanted to yank his hand away. Vierni wasn't her favorite—too loud for her, too chunky—but it was still a priceless piece of art that could be damaged by the oil in his skin.

She recognized the irony of that, since she herself had once gone viral on the feeds for hugging a priceless sculpture. But that'd been a very specific situation.

"I mean what do you *want*?" Striker said. "Not from the Federation, specifically."

"Money," she said.

Striker drummed his fingers on the Vierni's base. "You don't seem the type to drum up exorbitant gambling fees, though I admit your activities do surprise me regularly. And you must have the resources to pay your tuition or buy a home on any world you'd like. I know who your family is, of course. So what do you need the money for?"

There wasn't any need to hide it, not really. In fact, there was ample reason to tell him exactly what she was doing bouncing around the galaxy. She'd promised Hilda she'd do everything she could to find Vin. And that meant taking an occasional risk.

If Striker knew a bit more about her than she'd expected, well, she couldn't expect a man with the resources to detect invisible Fleet ships to be ignorant about her.

"I need to find my uncle," she said. "I have reason to believe he wasn't an outlaw at all, and that he worked undercover for the Federation."

"Yes." Striker let go of the sculpture and turned to face her. She had to resist the urge to whip out a tissue and clean the spots he'd touched. "We've searched for him. We continue to. He's like mist. Gone."

She licked her lips. That much, she knew. But some part of her had expected him to deny Vin's connection to the Federation altogether.

"I don't have to tell you who I suspect," Striker said.

He didn't have to tell her because he'd essentially accused Fortune himself, not ten minutes ago. If Striker thought she'd miss the way he'd been working her emotions back there, he was dead wrong. His accusations had clearly been designed for her to hear, as much as they had been for Fortune.

But could Fortune really be responsible for Uncle Vin's disappearance? He'd helped her fix *Moneymaker*'s engine, teaching her some of the basic mechanics as they'd worked. And he had a sense of humor, too. It was underdeveloped, sure, but it was there.

Also, and this was really the key point, Fortune seemed almost...too pure. For a man who commanded the only real military force in the galaxy, and who'd done so for as long as she could remember, he really did act almost naive at times.

"I know. He doesn't *seem* the type. So restrained. So proper." Striker said it as if in response to her thoughts, as if he could read her expressions. Or her thoughts themselves. Maybe there *was* some merit in Fortune's mask-like blankness. "But I assure you, Ms. Tarnish, that he can be as ruthless as any of the deadliest criminals in the galaxy. He's a dangerous man."

She thought of the way that Fleet frigate had blinked into sight beside *Moneymaker*. Fortune had lied to her by omission, and he continued to lie when he pretended the Fleet had nothing to do with Olton Moon. But hadn't she done the same to him?

Fortune certainly had the resources to make Vin disappear. If nothing else, she couldn't rule him out.

Striker had started walking again, and Sloane followed him past another trio of priceless paintings and out into the city, where a blue-green twilight was falling between the towers. Lights glittered on the streets, the blinking signs more inviting than ever as they advertised the city's shows, its food, its clubs.

Striker strode along beside her, his presence much different than the Commander's. He was easy and smiling, waving a hand to every other person they passed. "I would like to offer you a job, Ms. Tarnish."

She stumbled, and he shot out a hand to steady her. "I'm sorry?" she said. "Do you mean another bounty?"

"No. I mean a job. Believe it or not, most of our people work on salary." He gave her arm a squeeze, then let go. "First, though, I'd like to contract you to deliver Brighton to the bounty posters on Halorin. Then come back here, and we'll talk."

Sloane was shaking her head. "I can't. My ship is a mess, and—"

"We're already fixing the ship, free of charge—our thanks for bringing our attention to the Cal Cornum mess—and under your pilot's watchful eye. It'll be back to a hundred percent within a day." He stretched out a hand, sweeping his arm out as if to show off the city's glittering lights. As though to take credit for them. "Spend the night in the city. Visit a club, take it all in. Freic will let you know where you're staying. Tomorrow, take Brighton to Halorin, and we'll pay you double the original bounty."

They'd *double* the original bounty? Why? Why would they want to pay her so much to get Brighton back to a Center System? Surely they had other criminals waiting to be extradited to Halorin. Sloane wasn't the best at managing her own finances, but she was pretty sure this was a waste of money.

And why would they want to hire her, of all people?

"Don't you have transports for this sort of thing?" she asked.

Striker's grin widened. "Of course we do. Give it some thought, Ms. Tarnish. The Federation could use someone like you."

Before she could formulate a response, or point out that he hadn't answered her question, he tipped her a short bow, spun on his heel, and headed back in the direction of his office.

CHAPTER 19

"I DON'T UNDERSTAND why I have to come out with you." Alex had twisted her hair into two short braids that ended in little sprays at the base of her neck, and she was scowling so hard that it had to be uncomfortable. Didn't stop her from doing it, though. If she kept it up, her eyebrows were going to fuse with her nostrils.

Striker had put them up in a hotel near the center of the city, at least according to the map in Sloane's eye screen. There was certainly lots of activity there, the pristine streets giving off a glow of their own as music drifted out of fancy lobbies, the hov trains providing a background track of huffing clanks, like the crystal tones of a bell.

Everything about the city promised beauty, safety, and fun. It was almost like being back on Elter.

Their own hotel tower was purple, the room comfortably swathed in silky layers of black and pink. Hilda had stayed on the ship to keep an eye on the work, leaving Sloane with Alex—who'd immediately tried to burrow into the cushy hotel bed to order room service, no doubt with big plans to wallow.

Sloane had insisted she come out. And she could be incredibly persuasive.

Strong, too. Which Alex now knew, as she'd been dragged out of the bed and into the first non-PJ outfit Sloane could lay her hands on. You didn't have to dress to the nines to have a good time, but sometimes you needed a friend to remind you there was more to the world than wormholes and sadness.

Now, Sloane considered looping an arm through Alex's —for fun, not to keep the scientist from bolting, though the double purpose would work just fine—then decided the gesture probably wouldn't be welcome. She settled for what she hoped was an encouraging smile. "You needed to get out," she said. "What's the point of traveling the galaxy if you stay in your sad little lab all the time?"

"I was going to travel the entire *universe*," Alex said. "That was the plan."

Sloane risked elbowing Alex gently in the arm. It was time for Alex to stop sulking. Grieve the loss of her work, sure, but move on. Try something new. "So start here."

Alex rolled her eyes, an impressive feat with that scowl still on her face. "Fine."

The scientist wasn't exactly dressed for clubbing, in slacks and a high-necked blouse and which looked better suited for lounging than dancing. Then again, Obsidian City didn't seem to have a standard for after-hours dress. As soon as twilight faded into night, everyone in the city seemed to crowd into the street. The place was alive with glitter and smiles, with music that thrummed out of every open door and the sweet smells of flowered perfume and tropical drinks.

In a way, Obsidian City was almost suspiciously nice. Clean. Welcoming.

Or maybe Sloane had been bouncing through the Parse underworld for too long. She led Alex into the club the hotel concierge—a nice AI that'd spoken to them without even a hint of condescension—had recommended, and the scientist followed. Though not before heaving an enormous sigh.

"You'd think I was leading you to get your legs waxed or something," Sloane said.

"That sounds like more fun."

One step inside the club, and Sloane could see the AI had given them the perfect recommendation. The place was like the inside of a seashell, with pearly pink walls that'd been sculpted into dappled waves. Wide tiers defined the space, each layer lined with a long bar and a sprinkling of high-top tables that looked down over a dance floor. It felt almost like walking into an inverted cake.

"See?" Sloane said. "It's nice."

Alex wrinkled her nose. "It's very... pink."

"You say that like it's a bad thing."

Alex just stared at Sloane like she'd lost her mind. But she seemed to relax, at least a little, as they made their way to a table and ordered drinks from one of the serving drones that'd been designed to look like flying conch shells. When Sloane tried to pay, the drone informed her that she was on Striker's tab tonight.

"Does this guy have a first name?" Alex asked as the drone zipped away, taking a tentative sip of her soda. The drink was disconcertingly orange, and Sloane was afraid to ask what was in it.

Sloane's martini had come piled with booze-soaked pineapple, which she removed and set aside. College had taught her a few things, after all, and there was no need to make *that* mistake again. "Maybe Striker *is* his first name."

"Striker Smith," Alex said. "Sure. Why not?"

For some reason, the thought made Sloane laugh. "What is it with these guys?"

"You certainly seem to attract them."

Sloane's smile suddenly felt frozen on her lips, like someone had pasted it there without her permission, as Oliver's face drifted unbidden—unwelcome—into her thoughts. She did have a tendency to attract troublesome men. Maybe Oliver's memory had been bound to surface, after that meeting with Striker. They weren't alike—Oliver had been sandy-haired and muscular, where Striker's head looked like a matchstick.

Still, there was something there, and it brought Oliver rioting into her thoughts. She hated him for it.

She'd just have to add it to his list of crimes.

Alex didn't seem to notice. She slipped off her seat. "I need the bathroom. I'll be back."

With Alex gone, Sloane let the smile slip off her face and downed half her drink. Another, and her troubles with men might just start to blur.

As soon as the thought crossed her mind, a man in a dark suit sauntered into her space to lean his elbows on the table. Not on the opposite side, but just beside her. Close enough to elbow in the... Well, the knee, and other parts.

"You looked so beautiful when you were smiling," he said. "I wish you'd smile again."

Sloane tapped another drink order into the tabletop. "And I wish you'd buy some breath mints, but we can't all get what we want."

He frowned, then backed away from the table, hands raised as if she'd tried to shoot him. A smart one. Good.

The man hadn't been gone two seconds before a woman took his place. Sort of, anyway; she at least slid into Alex's empty seat instead of trying to encroach on Sloane's personal space.

The woman had on a strapless dress that showed off the geometric tattoos running up and down her arms, some of them creeping toward her shoulders. An Interplanetary Dweller. The woman's tattoos were shifting, pearlescent lines, a beautiful contrast to her ebony skin. Sloane couldn't tell if they were showing their own colors, or if they were programmed to reflect the light of the room.

When Sloane caught the woman's eye, she smiled, a slow spread of lips that'd been touched with light pink gloss.

"No offense," Sloane said, "but you saw that dude—I'm really not in the mood tonight."

Flattered, a little, but not in the mood. Not with Oliver drumming at her memories, and Striker's job offer. Not with Fortune's departure pushing a swirl of guilt through her stomach, like she ought to have made sure he'd made it safe to his ship.

No, she needed a few drinks and a good night's sleep. Or maybe a bit of feverish dancing. Wherever the night took her, though, it was not going to end in someone else's bed. That was just a recipe for disaster.

Text flickered across Sloane's eye screen, and she thought it must be Alex, maybe with a request to help her find their table. But this was new signal: one she didn't recognize. Sloane looked at the woman, who nodded.

This woman had bypassed the eye screen's security to send a direct message, without Sloane's authorization. It took a minute to let that sink in. There weren't many in the galaxy who could pull that off, and even fewer who would. Most *governments* didn't do that, even in emergencies.

It was one of those topics that came up repeatedly, at least where she'd grown up on Elter, whenever someone wanted to do a little posturing. Governments should be able to alert their people to immediate danger, one politician would say. And the inevitable answer? People have fliptabs, and the government can employ dozens of methods for important announcements, including drone deployment and, at least on domed worlds, sky signals. Sloane was inclined to agree.

Who *was* this woman, that she had the means to hack straight into Sloane's tech? Did she work for the Federation? For the Fleet?

Sloane started to be offended, to ask who this woman thought she was, when the content of the message registered in her mind. She paused, frowned, and pulled it up again, all while the woman waited patiently on the other side of the table.

I know where Vin stashed the data key.

Sloane blinked, allowed her mind to absorb the information. All right. The woman had her attention. "You know where my uncle is?"

The woman laid her hands on the table, palms flat, displaying elegantly manicured nails. The polish on them swirled, pulsing with the beat of the music. "No. But I know that the data you helped him steal never made it to the Federation. Do you find that strange, Ms. Tarnish?"

She had a lilting accent, one that Sloane couldn't quite place. Oliver had grown up with Interplanetary Dwellers, and he hadn't spoken in the same musical tones, but Sloane hadn't run across many others.

It *was* strange that the data key had never made it to the Federation. When she'd last seen Vin, he'd been ready to take it straight to them. To Striker himself, perhaps. Sloane didn't know what had happened, and she hadn't found any information in her uncle's room about what might have distracted him from that mission—or stopped him from completing it.

Hilda and Alex didn't know, either, which had always felt... wrong. Strange. Why hadn't he told his crew what he was doing?

"Ms. Tarnish?" the woman prompted, still watching her with open curiosity.

"Ms. Tarnish," Sloane repeated. "Why is everyone in this galaxy so stars-damned polite?"

First Fortune, then Striker, now this woman. She was getting sick of the sound of her own last name.

The woman smiled, a brief expression that was gone so quickly that Sloane might have imagined it. "I think you'd like to retrieve this data, Sloane. And I have need of your services. If you're willing, I'd like to offer you a job."

"Get in line. I'm a hot commodity apparently."

The woman sat back in the chair and crossed her legs. She looked casual—like a model taking a break from a shoot, a vid star on vacation—and yet something about her movements made her look dangerous, too. "Striker offered you a job, too, yes? But mine is more aligned with your interests. Not that you need to choose, Ms... Sloane. You might find it useful to spend some time in the Coordinator's company."

"In his pocket, you mean."

"Only if you allow that."

"Who are you?"

"You can call me Ivy."

"Is that your name?"

Ivy folded her hands in her lap. No answer, then. Not that Sloane had expected one.

Sloane licked her lips, scanning the room. Striker seemed to know everything that happened on his planet. He seemed to know everything that happened in the *galaxy*, though that couldn't be true. Could it? He'd thanked her for alerting him about the Cal Cornum situation, as if he hadn't known before, but that could have been a ruse.

"Don't worry," Ivy said. "Our conversation cannot be overheard. That is, anyone who overhears it will find themselves listening to something else entirely."

Sloane didn't know how that was possible, and she definitely wasn't about to trust this mystery woman on a word. "The job," she said. "Is it Federation approved?"

Ivy just looked at her, blinking long eyelashes. After a moment, she poured herself out of the chair, dress glimmering like a waterfall, and set a black rectangular card on the table. When Sloane picked it up, the words shimmered like its owner's tattoos. "Here's my contact information," Ivy said. "Get in touch after you drop your bounty in Halorin, and we'll talk."

"I haven't decided whether or not I'm going to... Wait, how do you know Striker asked me to go to Halorin?" She held up a hand. "You know what, never mind. I'll just assume everyone knows everything, all the time."

Except for her. Always except for her.

Ivy smiled again, holding it longer this time. "It's a good policy, overall. I'll be seeing you soon, yes?"

Without waiting for an answer, the woman glided into the crowd and disappeared.

CHAPTER 20

GARETH KNEW he needed to get back to the Adu System as soon as possible. Or in lieu of that, to deploy another pair of ships there while he stopped at his office in Cadence to do some digging. He hadn't quite decided which, but either way he should be moving. He had responsibilities, major ones, and he needed to see to them.

There was no reason to keep *Sabre* in the Pike System, not when the Federation had rejected his bid for negotiation. He couldn't imagine Striker would be open to speaking with him again.

But Gareth hadn't seen the *Moneymaker* leave the planet, either, and no matter how much he tried to convince himself otherwise, he couldn't help taking a sliver of responsibility for... for its crew. Not that she couldn't handle herself—that they couldn't handle themselves, that was— but they'd been on the ground on Cal Cornum, and Sloane had saved his life. If she had a target on her back because of it, that would be his fault.

So Gareth kept his fully crewed frigate waiting at the edge of the Pike System and hoped that Striker wouldn't get cranky about it. If nothing else, Gareth needed to assume that Striker, and the Federation by extension, knew what he was doing.

It would make subterfuge a lot harder, but he'd learned to work with facts rather than wishes. He kept *Sabre* circling close enough to the Current that it could make a quick exit if they ship was needed elsewhere—*when* it was needed; he was always expecting a call—but for now, he made sure to stay within watching distance of Federation. A full day had passed, by the Center System clocks most of the galaxy employed, and *Moneymaker* still hadn't left the planet.

He just wanted to at least know that she'd left unharmed. After that, he'd go.

And if she didn't emerge... Well, Striker would just have to host Gareth again. And this time, he'd bring a platoon along.

Gareth was standing on the bridge, watching some of the newer officers training on the control-deck protocols—stalled or not, he needed to make good use of his soldier's time—when Alisa March pinged his fliptab.

With a brief glance at the bridge, which was clicking efficiently along as usual, Gareth stepped into one of the adjoining meeting rooms to take her call. The room was fully equipped with a holo-table and projectable maps, but he brought her up on his fliptab, anyway. It felt more comfortable, somehow, and more private.

He didn't suspect his soldiers of spying. But Striker was getting his information somehow, so it was better to proceed with caution.

"I'm hearing rumors, Gareth," Alisa said, by way of a greeting. The Commission Representative had never been one for small talk. Maybe that was why they were friends. "Are they true?"

Gareth sat down on the edge of the table, angling himself so he could keep an eye out the sliver of window that looked out on the bridge, in case he was needed. He wouldn't be, not when he insisted on keeping his soldiers in this holding pattern—Sloane would be *fine* without him, she truly would —but it was best to stay within reach whenever possible.

"Depends," he said. "What do the rumors say?"

"That someone tried to have you killed on Cal Cornum."

"Then yes, they're true."

Alisa let out a string of curses, and he had to suppress a smile. She looked like a proper grandmother, with her hair tied back tight and her eyes surrounded in lines, but she could swear with the best of soldiers. "Are you all right?"

"Unscathed." Thanks to Sloane. Maybe *she* should be looking out for *him*. Though she'd made it clear she wouldn't take any job that associated her with the Fleet.

She couldn't really think he'd had a hand in her uncle's disappearance, could she?

"Any idea who's responsible?" Alisa asked.

Gareth watched as two of his soldiers paced into view outside the window, speaking animatedly. Discussing a vid they'd both seen, maybe, or a book. They looked happy, so it couldn't be about politics.

He liked to see his soldiers building up camaraderie like that. Maybe there was a way to encourage it even more. Make them feel more like a family. They shipped out together for months at a time, often not knowing when they'd next get planetside leave. It was worth considering.

Gareth returned his attention to Alisa, who was

watching him with narrowed eyes, as if she was considering reporting this whole situation to his mother. Who, if she did try that, would just tell Alisa matter-of-factly that it was part of the job and that Alisa ought to know it.

"I was on Cal Cornum because of Osmond Clay," he said. "Clay asked me to retrieve an employee who'd absconded with a load of data chips. But when I got there, I found the same employee had been tagged in an illegal bounty posting."

"Got crowded, did it?"

"You could say that. Suffice it to say the setup was a trap that began with hand cannons pointed at my head."

Alisa nodded. "Glad it didn't end there, Gareth.

"You and me both."

She didn't smile. "All right. But I'm still stuck on the fact that you agreed to do a job for Osmond Clay in the first place."

A job. It would be insulting, except for the fact that bounty hunters *had* come crashing after the exact same target. Clay had played him; there was no use ignoring it. "I agreed to assist him in a delicate matter," he said.

Alisa snorted. "And how many data chips were involved?"

Couldn't get much past Alisa. "A fair few."

He couldn't feel bad about that part of it. His father, like his mother, would have said that it was part of the job—that in order to run the Fleet, you needed the tools and materials. You couldn't feel bad about accepting them from those who wanted to provide them.

His father would have gone after Clay's employee, too. Though Dad probably would have exercised a bit more... caution. And Dad wouldn't have pissed Clay off in the first place.

Alisa leaned forward, propping her elbows on a surface in front of her and pressed her fingertips together. She must be sitting at the desk in her office, though it wasn't visible in the holo. "Let me just make sure I understand what I'm hearing. You think Osmond Clay, the lead producer of data chips in the galaxy and a respected member of the Fleet Advisory Commission, attempted to have you assassinated?"

"That's what I'm saying," Gareth said. "And I'll raise you one. I think the Cosmic Trade Federation knew about it."

Alisa sat back in her chair and covered her face with her hands. "My mother wanted me to become a dancer," she muttered. "Why didn't I listen to her?"

Gareth wasn't sure what to say to that, so he didn't respond. He watched as his soldiers finished their conversation and split off. He knew, without checking his watch, that it was almost shift-change time. The rotation might as well have been programmed into him; an internal rhythm as reliable as his own heartbeat.

"OK," Alisa said, dropping her hands back to her lap and leaning forward. All business again. "But you said this was only posted as an *illegal* bounty."

"Correct."

"Then I don't see how the Federation could be involved."

"Exactly. Maybe they wanted deniability."

She rolled her bottom lip between her teeth, then let it go. "Or maybe it's as simple as it looks, Gareth. Maybe whoever posted that bounty wanted to kill you and then clean up the loose ends by taking out the killer."

"But the bounty target wasn't the assassin, so why send him there at all?"

"To give you someone to track."

Fair enough. If Clay had fed him the information, he'd have gotten suspicious. "The cartels wouldn't dare."

Wouldn't they, though? The Callows and the Mechics had ganged up on *Sabre* back in Adu, an unprecedented posturing. But with the Bone System sliding further and further into criminally charged anarchy, it might well become the new norm.

Alisa cleared her throat. "You've been saying it yourself, Commander. The cartels are out of control. I wouldn't rule them out."

It wasn't impossible. It was unlikely, but it wasn't impossible. Assassinating the Fleet Commander could, in theory, throw the organization into disarray—though Gareth was confident in the integrity of the chain of command. Still, even a beat of hesitation on the Fleet's part could turn the whole system into a permanent chaos zone.

That didn't explain everything, though. Not even close.

"But why did Clay send me there, if he wasn't involved?" Gareth asked. "Even if you leave out the Federation, it still comes down to him."

Alisa cursed again, though she kept it short this time. "It's a heavy accusation, Gareth. A very heavy accusation. We need to buy some time until we can investigate. And you need to get back to the Adu System."

Didn't he know it? But he couldn't leave Pike until he knew Sloane was on her way, too. He didn't trust Striker, and he didn't trust the Federation. They could make her disappear.

He shouldn't have left her behind.

As if on cue, Lager appeared in the window and raised a hand to beckon him onto the bridge.

"Will do, Alisa," Gareth said. "I have to go."

"Back to Adu, I hope," she said. Before he could respond, she ended the call.

It wasn't exactly the outcome he'd hoped for. He'd wanted her to be outraged, and she was, but she still saw Clay as a minor annoyance from a minorly-powerful Outer System that wanted to throw its weight around like a Middle System. She didn't see him as a murderer.

Gareth knew better.

He closed his fliptab with a snap and joined Lager at the door. "Lieutenant?"

"Stills got a lock on *Moneymaker*, sir. Ship's leaving orbit and heading for the Halorin Current."

Gareth followed Lager out onto the bridge, watching as the Lieutenant pulled up *Moneymaker*'s estimated trajectory on the viewport. *Sabre* was too far for him to make out a real-view visual of her ship; it was just a spark of light in the distance. But it was there.

Halorin. That was interesting. Why would Sloane want to head back to the Center Systems? She seemed pretty settled on the mercenary lifestyle, and he realized that some part of him had been expecting them to be taking similar paths back toward the Adu System.

It was better this way, really. She didn't belong in the Bone System. Though knowing Sloane, she was probably only heading out to Halorin to get her ship fixed. And avoiding Elter, too, so she wouldn't run into her father.

As he watched, *Moneymaker*'s signature arched toward the Current, intercepted it, and disappeared.

There. She was gone. Time to move on.

Lager was watching Gareth, with a gleam in his eye that said he was holding back a comment. Gareth cleared his throat. "Set a bearing for Adu," he said. "We need to rendezvous with *Cutlass* and see whether..."

Gareth trailed off as a trio of ships zipped out of Federation's orbit and made a dash for the Current. Before he could check their signatures, three more followed, and another three, until there was an entire swarm of the things diving into the Current. He increased the zoom until the viewport told him exactly what types of ships they were.

Every single one of them had the tucked-in wings of the Fox Clan ships that'd attacked them when they'd entered Pike.

Gareth propped his palms on the railing as the ships poured after the *Moneymaker*. What would happen, when they caught up with her? In-Current attacks were rare, but those ships would chase Sloane right into Halorin. *That* many ships? They'd obliterate her in no time.

Lager still had that same foolish gleam in his eye. "Change of course, sir?"

Gareth leaned on the railing, watching as the ships vanished one by one into the flow of the Current. "Halorin System," he said. "And hurry."

CHAPTER 21

THERE WAS no way a System could look fancier than any other when viewed from space, but Sloane always thought Halorin System managed it, anyway. She'd only visited a couple of times before this—her father hadn't been big on far-flung vacations—and the place always seemed to have an extra bit of... sparkle. As if someone had polished Halorin itself and arranged its orbiting planets like jewels in a crown.

Or maybe it was just the System's reputation that gave it that extra glow. It was home to the most luxurious station in the galaxy, where celebrities famously mixed and mingled, and several resort-only moons that featured equator-wide beaches. She'd always wanted to visit one of those.

As she watched their entrance into the System from the sideport in the kitchen, she couldn't help thinking that it was really very beautiful.

She hadn't slept well, even in the cushy bed in the Obsidian City hotel Striker had booked for her. The conversation with Ivy had haunted her all night, making her toss and turn as she'd tried to replay every comment, every movement. The information on Ivy's card was sparse, and Sloane had no way of knowing who she worked for.

She couldn't trust anyone. Alex and Hilda, sure, but not Striker, and certainly not Ivy. The woman didn't want to find Vin out of the goodness of her heart, so why?

Until Sloane knew the answer, she needed to tread carefully.

"Your father wants to talk to you!" BRO said, snapping her into the present, his voice piping in from the ceiling, and Sloane sighed. Did Dad have some kind of alert that activated whenever she set foot—or spaceship—into a Center System?

"Way to ruin the view." Sloane pulled out her fliptab, with every intention of silencing yet another call from her father, but there was nothing on it. "He's not calling me."

"No, he's comming the ship!" BRO said. "Maybe he thought you'd actually answer!"

"Take a message," Sloane said. "And don't judge me."

"I'm already conversing with him! He just called me a hairless fist of wires! Is that good? I don't even have a body, so it's accurate, though it seems unnecessary to point it out."

Sloane snorted. "No, Dad makes up his own nonsense curses. And insults, sometimes. The angrier he is, the more ridiculous they get."

And off color, too. Or so he seemed to think. Did her mother still roll her eyes at those? Did her little sister still hide a giggle behind the back of her hand? Lissie must be getting big by now. How long had it been since Sloane had seen her?

Too long, if she had to wonder.

"Oh!" BRO said. "How angry was that one, do you think?"

"I'd say about a seven out of ten."

"Oh! Well, in that case..." BRO trailed off, and for a moment she thought it was focusing on the conversation with her father—though that was silly, really, since an AI could hold on more than one conversation at once.

To be fair, most AIs could do that. BRO was... special.

When it stayed silent for a full minute, Sloane frowned. BRO liked to talk—the trick was getting it to shut up—and she hadn't expected it to drop the conversation completely.

"Hello?" Sloane tapped the side of the ship, which Fortune would probably laugh at her for, though that assumed the Commander was capable of laughter. The AI didn't have nerves, and she couldn't jumpstart it into talking with a good wham, but whatever. Fortune didn't know everything. "Are you there?"

"A triangle," BRO said, "is perpendicular to a fornicating shovel!"

Sloane sighed. "Yeah, I'd say that's more like a nine out of ten for Dad. New grammatical structure, though. He's changing it up."

The ship rocked, hard, and Sloane went flying across the kitchen table, landing head-first on the booth with her feet still splayed over it. When she righted herself, the booth was briefly on the floor, gravity pulling her sideways. At least, as opposed to the normal ways.

"Sloane," Hilda's voice rang into her ear from somewhere—the ceiling, her ear, she was all mixed up. "We've got Fox Clan."

Great. That was just great. Sloane unfolded herself from the booth and slid out onto the floor, grateful that no one was there to see her. She pushed herself up as the ship lurched again, staggering toward the short bridge that connected the kitchen to the pilot's deck.

"BRO," she said, "prepare the weapons systems, will you?"

"The purple rainbow wants to simulate the brothel!" BRO said.

"OK, tell Dad he's gross and hang up. We've got bigger problems."

The ship shuddered as if in response, though she wished it wasn't quite so eager to reinforce her point. Her stomach jumped, and she swallowed hard, willing her gourmet Obsidian-City breakfast to stay put as Hilda maneuvered.

"Brighton!" BRO said. "The knotted hairless wires are from Brighton! The doors are gaping with—"

"Do not finish that sentence," Sloane said. "Are you trying to tell me Brighton's messing with you?"

"Okra!"

"I'll take that as a yes." Sloane grabbed onto a storage shelf and used it to swing herself back in the opposite direction. Hilda didn't need her help on the pilot's deck, not really, so Sloane would have to go deal with Brighton. Or at least fix the damage he'd done.

She hauled herself across the line of shelves as the ship dipped and curved, Hilda hopefully using her ace-pilot skills to get them out of this mess. When she took a particularly hard turn, Sloane narrowly kept from slamming her head on the shelf. Why did she somehow always find herself diving through Uncle Vin's stars-damned ship with Fox Clan dragon ships on her ass? She should've asked Striker for enhanced shields. And a retirement package.

She started through the kitchen with the intention of using the spiral staircase to drop down into the cargo bay. Before she could start down, though, a light in the med bay caught her attention. It was too bright, as if one of the side-ports had been opened back there.

Of course, she shouldn't be able to see anything if the pod were still attached to the end of the med bay, the way it should be.

Using the frame of the door for leverage, Sloane pulled herself into the med bay, ignoring BRO's senseless yammering and Hilda's shouting in her ear.

One of the escape pods was indeed dropping away from *Moneymaker,* the sight crystal clear through the now open sideport. Thoughtful of Brighton, to leave her a window.

The little pod zipped through the thick cluster of Fox Clan ships. There were so *many* of them, their wings tucked into their sides, noses aimed at *Moneymaker.* They had her surrounded. Like a bug in a jar.

All at once, it seemed like Hilda's constant maneuvering wasn't nearly enough. They'd never face down this many ships. Even with their shields at full capacity, *Moneymaker* wouldn't last long.

Yes, alerts would be going off all over the Halorin System, security protocols would be activating, ships no doubt zooming out of atmo to meet the threat. By the time help got here, it'd be too late.

Not for Brighton, though. Somehow, the little pod was pinging through the cluster of enemy ships with ease. They ignored him.

"Sorry, kid." Now *Brighton* was in her ear, and she had a feeling the guy was still using her own comm system to talk to her. Or overriding BRO somehow. "I can't stay."

It was kind of insulting, given that he'd clearly been capable of busting out of that crate this whole time. He could have escaped well before this, and he hadn't bothered.

He'd been waiting for her to make a move. And now, he'd hacked her AI into near uselessness.

Still, that pod looked like a mouse dashing through a den of cats. Defenseless. She didn't want Brighton to die. Get punched a little, maybe but not die. "Fox Clan's attacking us," she said. "They'll take you out, too. You've got no shield, no guns. Nothing."

Brighton barked a deep, humorless laugh. "They're too busy with you to bother with me. *You* stole their bounty and handed it over to the CTF. Short attention spans, these guys. Besides, I tweaked the signals so this looks like a bot ship. No one inside."

Sloane swallowed hard, fighting to keep the bile from rising into her throat. "That's a useful skill."

"Very. Anyway, I figure I'd rather not die there, no offense, and I'm definitely not going to rot in a prison on Halorin."

"I hear they've got really lux ones."

"Nevertheless. You're on your own, kid."

She wanted to say that she'd thought they were friends, but the words dried on her tongue. He'd been her prisoner, a legal bounty, but not a friend. She would have turned him in, no questions asked.

Brighton might be a good conversationalist, and he might've stood up for her with Bellow, but he wasn't her uncle. He was just another man, and he was doing what they did best: first betraying her, and then running away.

The ship swayed. "I cannot keep this up forever," Hilda said in her ear.

"Sure you can," Sloane said, trying to sound like she believed it. "You're an amazing pilot."

"There are dozens of those ships. Maybe a hundred. They followed us right out of Pike."

Yes, she could see that. Where had they been hiding, that Striker hadn't known they were there?

Or maybe he *had* known. Yet another name for the not-a-friend list.

"Then shoot at them," Sloane said.

"I'd love nothing more, but Brighton took out the guns."

The guns. The pod. The AI. What *had* he left her with?

Sloane wanted to cry, or hit the ship, or both. But none of those things would save their lives.

Gritting her teeth, she wrenched herself away from the window and headed for engineering, hoping her newfound mechanical knowledge would be enough to fix the guns. Even though Fortune hadn't shown her the guns, or even mentioned them. No doubt for good reason.

To be fair, they hadn't been *fixing* the guns at the time, but at the moment, she wasn't exactly inclined to feel kindly toward any men who acted friendly.

She scanned her palm against the door and staggered into the engineering room as *Moneymaker* lurched, hard enough to spin her straight into the wall. She pushed forward, anyway, bracing her hand along the wall.

Even with the ship jerking her around at every step, the smell of grease and metal was grounding. Not quite comforting, but almost. She wasn't a gearhead, but for a second, she thought she got it. She took a long breath, and then another. Brighton had left in a hurry. He was a good hacker, but she knew this ship. She could fix it.

A blast tore through her eardrums, reverberating in her ribcage, and the floor dropped out from under her. She went flying toward the rail, her body sliding between the metal slats without her permission as the ship flipped.

Her legs slammed against the side of the reactor casing, but she ignored the blast of pain from the hit and hooked her elbow around the rail to catch herself before she could fall the rest of the way. Her arm jolted, a quick warning shot of pain, but it stopped her forward momentum, so there was still reason to be optimistic about her chances.

The ship spun again, and she cried out as her elbow took on her full weight, her body nearly slipping before she managed to clench the fingers of her left hand around the rail to relieve some of the pressure.

Still, sparks erupted across her vision as pain cracked through the right side of her body, hot and fierce. If that arm wasn't broken, she'd be shocked.

The ship spun a third time, and she held onto the rail, legs flailing. Alarm lights flared across her vision, though she couldn't hear the accompanying bells. Either the blast had been that loud, or the sounds were out. Neither could be good.

That was a hit. Hilda's words were blurry but legible as they streamed across Sloane's eye screen while she hung there, gulping in air, trying to use her good arm to pull herself back up onto the platform. *They bypassed our shields. Better suit up.*

CHAPTER 22

BETTER SUIT UP. Easier said than done, when Sloane was dangling from the rail in engineering from one good hand and one broken arm.

A direct drop to the next level wouldn't have been so bad, under normal circumstances. Ten feet, maybe. But the ship was spinning, either by Hilda's design or because it was out of control, and if she let go, she could end up falling all the way to the bottom of the ship—she didn't want to estimate that drop—or end up bouncing between various bits of dangerous machinery.

Yeah, it wasn't good.

But those alarms were still flashing, and Hilda's instructions blinked like a time bomb on her eye screen. How long did she have? Her lungs were already burning, and it was impossible to tell whether that was because of the exertion, the pain, or the failing life support systems.

"Pick one," she muttered. She tightened her good hand's grip on the rail—it was dewy with condensation now, a bad sign in the realm of life support—and pulled.

The ship spun again, and her feet went up over her

head. Her injured arm felt like it was on fire; it took every ounce of will in her possession not to yank it away from the rail.

Why aren't you suiting up? Hilda's text streamed across her vision, and she wanted to rip the eye screen out to get rid of the distraction.

I'm a little busy trying not to die.

Well hurry up, or you'll die anyway.

Sloane wished she could believe the pilot was exaggerating. But her lungs were definitely working harder now, and it was from more than the rigorous not-dying exertions. *I could use some help.*

I'll call the security officer. Oh, wait, you bought a defective AI instead.

This really isn't the time. Can you keep the ship steady for thirty seconds?

You've got five. Starting now.

Gritting her teeth, Sloane pulled. Tears streamed down her face, and her sore throat told her she was yelling in pain, but she didn't stop pulling until she heaved herself up over the rail and back onto the platform.

It felt like thirty minutes, but it must've been within Hilda's five seconds. The ship banked again, and she held on.

When she survived this, she was going to replace those gap-filled rails with slabs of aluminum siding.

Sloane crawled to the emergency cabinet, smashed it open, and pushed past the pain in her arm to rip a helmet out. She yanked it onto her head, engaged the seals, and took a deep breath of sweet, sweet O2. She hadn't realized how dense the air was getting.

A comm chimed in the helmet, and she would have been relieved to have her hearing intact—those alarm lights still blazed silently overhead—had her right arm not been dangling uselessly at her side.

The comm channel said the message was from another ship. The *Sabre* was requesting a connection.

She didn't know the *Sabre*... except she was pretty sure she did. Sloane leaned back against the wall, taking another long breath before reaching for the rest of the suit. She had a feeling she was going to need it.

And then she accepted the comm. "My god, Fortune," she said, "could you have named your ship anything more testosterone-fueled? Size doesn't matter, you do know that."

There was a beat of silence. She supposed he could have had one of his officers staffing the comms, but somehow she knew he didn't. And then he said, "Could you have named your ship anything more mercenary?"

"Probably, but I didn't name my ship."

"And I didn't name mine."

Sloane pulled her legs into the bottom of the suit, then braced her back against the wall and used it to help her up so she could slip her good arm into the sleeve. The other one was going to be painful. "You know, for a military body that aims to promote peace, you've got violent ship names. I'm just saying."

"That's because no one would take us seriously if we showed up in a ship called the *Cupcake*."

Sloane actually laughed at that, which shook her shoulders and ended up sounding more like a gasp of pain. "Fortune," Sloane said, "did you just make a joke?"

"Don't get used to it." She was surprised to realize she could hear the concern in his voice. He had to have heard that gasp. "You sound... Are you all right?"

She didn't want to ask for his help, but she didn't see what other choice she had. There were times for pride, and there were times for not dying. This was most certainly the latter.

"Yeah, about that," Sloane said, "I'm kind of hoping your testosterone-fueled ship might be somewhere nearby. And willing to bully some Fox Clanners out of, I don't know, killing us."

"Your guns are still down?"

Sloane eased the second sleeve up over her injured arm, wincing as she finished the cuff. She zipped up the suit and activated the seals for full pressure. "They *were* up, but Brighton took them down again. He left in a hurry. Broke the AI. I'm in engineering."

"With your ship cartwheeling like that?"

Leave it to him to know exactly what that meant. "Affirmative, Commander. I've been bouncing around in here like a kernel of popcorn. Now are you going to help me, or just judge me?"

"I'm not— Okay." He took a breath, and she could almost *hear* the Commander side kicking in. If he called her 'soldier,' she intended to riot. "Your plasma cannons are an add-on, something your uncle built onto the existing structure of the freighter. Your AI wouldn't control them."

"Why not?"

"Because your uncle is a smart man, and he knows better than to bridge the central ship systems with the weapons, especially in a modular vessel like his. They'd be separate. Trust me on that."

Sloane leaned back against the wall again, heart skipping, arms shaking with the effort of ignoring the pain. "You're talking about Uncle Vin in the present tense. You don't think he's dead."

"Yes, well, I'm an optimist."

Or he knew exactly where Vin was. But for some

reason, Fortune wanted to help her, or at least to keep her alive. So she wouldn't question it. For now.

"Your weapons programming is at the bottom of the spiral," Fortune said. "If Brighton took off in a hurry, I'm betting he just flipped a switch."

"You scoped the weapons out when you were on the ship."

"I'm an optimist *and* a realist."

Sloane pushed herself back up to standing and followed his directions, taking the steps carefully and bracing herself against the left side railing with her good hand. She needed to hurry, but if she fell again, she'd never be able to get back up. Every step jolted her arm with a new bolt of pain. "You also seem like an enthusiast."

"Possibly."

She was going to need to remember, if she survived this, that the Commander gave much more away in the tone of his voice than he ever did with his face.

The ship banked, shuddering as more hits flicked against the sides of the ship. Sloane slammed into the opposite wall, hissing in a sharp breath as her broken arm jostled. The suit was poor protection for the injury.

"You're hurt," Fortune said. It sounded like an accusation. "You said you were all right."

"You asked if I was all right. I didn't answer."

He paused, as if replaying the conversation in his mind. Or maybe he was *literally* replaying their conversation. She could see him recording this. "Tell me again why you're not shooting at them yet?"

"I *am* shooting at them," he said. "Why do you think you're not dead? But there are a lot of them, and your ship is right in the thick of it."

Right. Wouldn't want to die from friendly fire. Not that

Fortune was friendly. He was just... not currently her enemy.

Sloane stepped down onto the bottom level of the engineering bay. "I'm here. Now what?"

"Vin had the weapon controls installed in a metal trunk. It's welded into the center of the floor."

"If I see him again, I'll make sure to tell him it's an inconvenient spot."

"Agreed. Your palm scan will open the top of the box."

Sloane dropped to her knees and placed her suit-shielded palm against the panel in the top. The box clicked open. "How did *you* get it open?"

"Same way Brighton did, I imagine."

She waited, but he didn't say anything more. "Are you going to enlighten me?"

"No. Now check the controls."

The box was *full* of controls. Bundled wires and zigzagging switches and blinking red-and-green lights, it was a mishmash of tech that she didn't understand. Chips and cords and all. Not for the first time, she wondered what the hell she was even doing here.

But she didn't realize her addled brain had spoken the question out loud until Fortune said, "You are looking for your uncle. And you're going to find him. The next step in that process is to check the controls."

He sounded certain. How could he sound so damned *certain*?

There were tears leaking down her cheeks, and they really needed to stop, because they were making her vision blurry. The helmet sucked away the moisture, but she couldn't wipe her nose, and it was annoying.

"I don't know what I'm looking at." She swallowed,

hoping Fortune wouldn't be able to hear the tears in her voice, though she suspected he probably could.

"Look for a disconnected cord, or a switch that's flipped to red. They should be green."

The ship rocked, and she used her knees to brace herself against the side of the control box. Cradling her injured arm to her chest, she reached her left hand into the box and sifted through the wires. "There," she said. "Loose end."

"Now find the empty slot."

She shifted the wires aside, peering in close. "There are two empty slots."

"One for plasma, one for missiles. You've got both."

"No rail gun?"

"Your ship would tip over. No rail gun. Plasma's usually green, laser's orange. Match those in."

Sounded simple enough. Or would have been, if any of the wires had been color coded. "They're all gray," she said. "Every single one."

"Got a knife?"

Yes, but she probably shouldn't use it with her atmo suit keeping her alive and her hands shaking like this. Still, she didn't see much of an option. She fumbled into the emergency toolkit at her waist, withdrew a small blade, and crouched down, her hurt arm screaming at her as she extended it so she could hold the wires steady.

"Not to rush you," Hilda said, "but where the *hell* are you?"

Sloane's hand slipped, and she pricked the fingertip of her suit. The material immediately spit out a glob of patching liquid, and she let out a long breath, steadying the blade.

"All the time in the world." Fortune's voice was steady,

calm. He'd probably been in a worse battle before breakfast. "Keep going."

To Sloane's surprise, Hilda didn't argue.

With pain ratcheting up her arm, Sloane held the wires down and sliced into the gray coating.

One wire was green. The other was orange. She swallowed back a sob of relief, forced the wires into their spots, and watched as the lights turned green.

"I did it," she said. She was pretty sure the sob was audible this time, a bubble in the back of her throat, but she didn't care. "Guns should be live."

"Affirmative," Hilda said. "Now get your ass up here."

Sloane half expected Fortune to bark at Hilda, but he didn't. Not his soldier to command, apparently. At least he knew it.

With her legs shaking and black spots crowding the sides of her vision, Sloane pushed herself back up onto her feet. Blood pulsed into her head, but she ignored the sensation as she ran up the spiraling lamp, protecting her injured arm against her chest as best she could.

She pushed through the med bay and made her way through to the pilot's deck.

As soon as she arrived, Alex jumped up out of the copilot's seat as if it had burned her. Sloane expected the scientist to abandon the flight deck altogether, but Alex pressed her lips together—like she might be sick, which Sloane could not blame her for—and dropped into the jumpseat.

Sloane strapped in, trying to hide her injury, but Hilda took one look at her and went white. "Sorry," she said.

Sloane couldn't hide her surprise. An apology, from Hilda? And for what? Saving their asses? Trying to hurry Sloane when they were under attack and leaking atmo?

"No reason to be," Sloane said.

Outside the viewport, a beautiful rainbow of missiles went spiraling out from *Moneymaker*, sending a handful of Fox Clan ships up in pretty little balls of flame. The Fleet frigate was firing, too—she couldn't believe his ship was called the *Sabre*, she really couldn't—and the thick swarm of Clan ships was getting thinner.

"We might just win this," Sloane said.

She really shouldn't have said it. As soon as the words left her mouth, a new ship poked its nose out of the Current.

And then it kept coming. And coming. Beside it, Fortune's frigate looked like a dolphin keeping company with a whale; this ship would dwarf a decent-sized moon. She didn't know how the Current could hold the whole thing, though she was admittedly vague on how Current tech worked in the first place.

"Tell me that's one of yours, Fortune," Sloane said.

The Commander took a very long moment to respond. When he did, there was an edge to his voice she hadn't heard before. "Negative. Not one of ours."

When the rest of the ship emerged, it was at least clear whose side they were on. It soared out of the Current with starlight wings extended, no doubt drinking in Halorin's rays for power. It looked like a dragon mother, surrounded by her children.

And when it extended its cannons, it was absolutely clear that the dragon meant to kill them all.

CHAPTER 23

GARETH COULDN'T IMAGINE where the Fox Clan had been hiding a ship like this. Even in Adu System, with its lawless chaos, it would be difficult to hide something of this magnitude. But it was easy to forget that Parse was a big galaxy, which plenty of hidden pockets and supposedly uninhabited systems. In truth, the galaxy hid all kinds of secrets.

Gareth had lived on ships all his life, and he knew better than to trust visual data alone. Especially out in the vacuum, where everything was distorted as his brain worked to put the vastness into context. This ship, though... The wings alone looked longer than *Sabre*'s entire length measured bow to stern.

Soldiers were already pounding the decks as Lager issued a stream of orders, the Lieutenant giving him a chance to think. To form a strategy.

Gareth didn't have one. "Closest backup?" he asked.

Stills was working the monitors again, sitting directly below where he stood on the bridge. "Cadence, sir. We've been so focused on Adu..."

Didn't he know it.

In his ear, Sloane's voice came through. "Didn't you say you've got some fancy stun net that can disable these ships?"

He coughed out a laugh. It caught painfully in his throat, like a hook. "Not a ship that size. And likely not in these numbers."

"In *some* numbers, though?"

Gareth pulled up the battle map on the viewport. It was less satisfying to watch the small ships blinking out of existence when one hit from the huge one could very well kill *Sabre*, and the three thousand souls aboard, in a blink. "You're right in the middle of them. You'll get disabled, too."

"I've got an ace pilot on my side, Fortune. But we'll *pretend* to get disabled."

In the background, Hilda asked a question. Gareth didn't hear Sloane's response, though it sounded something like *you'll figure it out.*

"Another stunt?" he asked.

Sloane sighed. "Do me a favor, Fortune. Send out your zappy disabling ships and do your best. Oh, and if you can catch that little pod Brighton's in, I'd be grateful."

At least she sounded like herself again. There was something... extra in her voice, like a low note of pain or an extra breath breaking up each sentence, and he wanted to stare through the comm until he understood how injured she actually was.

If she was telling a joke, she might not be in mortal danger. But then again, he had a feeling the last words this woman ever spoke would be flippant ones.

Gareth nodded to Lager, and the Lieutenant deployed the pilots. "And after we disable their ships? What will you do then? Invite them out for a drink? Plan a conspiracy together?"

Footsteps echoed through the background of her comm, and all around him as his soldiers rushed to follow orders. Gareth gripped the rail, forcing himself not to go after them, not to strap himself in a pod himself. In this case, his absence from the bridge *would* be a liability.

His soldiers could handle it.

"Give me some credit, Fortune," Sloane said. She was breathing hard, like she was moving. What was the woman doing? Moving to med bay, he hoped. "You pretend to retreat. They'll come for the supposedly disabled *Money-maker*. We'll fire directly into the bay they open, once we're inside the shield."

"You'll get caught *behind* their shield."

"Not if I hit the shield controls directly."

She was bold. He had to give her that. "If I could coordinate a way for the *correct* bay door to open so you could shoot your missile and hit the *correct* quadrant of their engineering bay, I would," he said. "But it's impossible."

"You sure?"

"Positive." He paused. "But I'm listening."

"Good. Plan B, then. But I'll need you to trust me. Can you?"

Could he? Sloane had saved his life on Cal Cornum when she could have stayed up on the hill and out of danger. She'd lied to him about the bounty being Federation approved—a lie of omission still counted, especially since he'd paid to fix her ship because of it—but he'd lied to her, too, and he should have checked the details of her bounty himself.

If nothing else, Fox Clan had been trying to kill her for

days now. They weren't likely to negotiate; she had no reason to turn on him.

Unless there was an illegal bounty on *his* head now. Best not to contemplate that.

"Pilots ready to deploy," Lager said.

There wasn't any way to be sure. Not a hundred percent. He was just going to have to trust her.

Gareth gave the order himself. "Lock the stun nets to disable."

The pilots chorused their understanding, and the ships shot out of *Sabre*'s bays, heading for the smaller Fox Clan ships. And the *Moneymaker*, which was still in the thick of the battle.

If the big ship fired... But no, if it fired on his pilots, it risked hitting its own. It *would* hit some of its own, without question. He couldn't believe even a criminal cartel like Fox Clan would be that cold. If nothing else, every ship represented a few million tokens they'd need to replace.

"Good job, Fortune," Sloane said, only just audible over a background soundtrack of rustling and clanging. What *was* she doing? "I'm proud."

On the viewport, the pilots locked their nets together and went fishing for Fox Clanners. Just as the stun nets passed through the biggest section of the swarm—the nets looked like bolts of lightning from here—Brighton's pod zipped out of the line of fire and dove toward the Current, slipping straight past the disabling net. All around the pod, Fox Clan ships went dark, their rockets blinking gloriously into nothingness, but Brighton's little light stayed frustratingly bright.

Curiously, though, Brighton's pod didn't disappear *into* the Current. Maybe the pod wasn't Current worthy, but then what did the fugitive hope to achieve by escaping in it?

As for *Moneymaker*, it went still. Very, very still. No lights. No nothing. "I very much hope that we did not capture your ship in that sweep," Gareth said, though if the ship *had* been caught, the comms would be out, too.

With its ships disabled, and ostensibly the *Moneymaker*, too, the huge dragon ship turned on the frigate.

"Make as if to retreat," Gareth ordered. That was what she'd said, so he'd do it, but he wouldn't go far. "But do it slowly."

Lager nodded. He wouldn't question orders, not up here on the bridge, but the question was there in his eyes.

There was a beat of silence while *Sabre* put a unit of distance between them and the Clan ship—Fleet-ship silence, which was still filled with footsteps and clacking keyboards and whispered communications—and while the stun-pilots brought their ships in to safety.

Gareth watched *Moneymaker*, through the viewport rather than the sim screen. What the hell was she planning? She didn't think Halorin System security would clean up this mess, did she? The Center Systems left their messes for the Fleet. And he wasn't at all sure the Fleet had a big enough mop for this one.

A second beat passed, and another pod slipped away from *Moneymaker*'s side and headed straight for the hulking Fox Clan ship.

Gareth's throat felt dry. "Lager, are there guns on that pod?"

"Affirmative, sir."

He trusted her. He had to. But she was heading straight for the enormous Fox Clan ship, and he still recalled her original plan with perfect clarity. If she couldn't use *Moneymaker*'s guns to take out the shields, she could still use the weapons on that pod. But the plan was rife with the same problems—she'd get trapped unless she could shoot straight to the shields, a long shot at best—and now her guns were *smaller*.

Gareth stared at the screen, willing her plan to crystal-ize. Willing himself to understand. "She wouldn't."

Lager cleared his throat. "With respect, sir, I think she just did."

CHAPTER 24

SLOANE HAD HOPED the Fox Clan's dragon-mother ship would be eager enough to have her as a guest that they'd refrain from shooting at her as she approached. And so far, as her little pod passed through the graveyard of deactivated ships, zooming close enough to some to see that the people were alive and well inside, though probably freaking out—Fortune's stun nets worked as well as he said—the dragon mother did nothing to stop her.

Of course, her pod might bounce back when she reached their shield. Or get caught in a stun net like Fortune's, though she'd never seen anyone else use a weapon like that.

She didn't know a lot about space battles, but she did know that most shields allowed ships to get in and out. On a case-by-case basis, of course.

Hers might be a no-dice case. But Fortune had trusted her, had helped her without knowing her full plan, so she had to try. She hadn't thought he had it in him. Maybe there was hope for the guy.

She didn't dare comm him, or Hilda, either. This close

to the dragon mother, the Clan might well be able to pick up their call, even if she used a secure frequency. So, she drifted forward in silence, managing to restrain a cheer when she made it past the shield perimeter without a problem. The pain helped with that; she felt like someone had tried to rip her arm out of its socket by strapping it to the underside of a hov-train.

As soon as she made it past the shield, the dragon-mother ship opened a comm to her. No ship ident, unfortunately. She'd have to keep calling it Dragon Mother.

"If you've come to negotiate, you're going to be disappointed," her Fox Clan welcome-committee said. He had a deep voice, gravelly, like he'd been swallowing rocks.

"Open a bay for me, and we'll talk."

"Hard to talk with a plasma bolt in your face."

"If you were going to shoot me, you'd have done it already."

That was only fifty-fifty, to be honest—she was still close enough to the other Clan ships that it would've been a risk for them to use one of those big fat guns on her. Now, though, she was inside the shields. They could open a bay and shoot a hand cannon at her without risking their people.

As she contemplated whether they'd try it, the closest set of bay doors parted, like the world's most ominous party invitation. When no hand cannons appeared, Sloane grinned and directed the pod straight for the bay. She wasn't a pilot—she only knew the basics—but she didn't need to be.

The bay was everything she'd expect to see from a regular transport station. She steered the pod between the walls and through the atmo-shield they'd engaged to keep the bay pressurized while ships came and went.

Instead of bringing her pod in for a graceful landing in the middle of the bay, Sloane gunned it straight through the far wall.

Surprised Fox Clanners scattered in every direction, but she hardly registered them as the egg-shaped pod exploded into the Dragon Mother's corridor. Glass and metal sprayed harmlessly against the pod's windshield, falling away with the sound of pattering rain. Almost pleasant from here. Bless Uncle Vin and his paranoia; the man had built some strong little accessories.

She'd gone into this assuming the corridors would be wide enough for a pod. The plan would still work if she had to scrape along the ceilings, but she might have ended up wedged into a corner.

Luckily, the Dragon Mother had luxuriously wide halls, almost sweeping. Striker himself might have designed them to impress would-be employees. The pod soared through easily, even under her questionable piloting.

It was nice to be right.

Now that she was inside—very much inside, and still sending surprised cartel members leaping out of the way as she bumped along through the corridor—she opened comms. "OK, Fortune," she said, "which way to the shield controls?"

The pod cracked into the right wall and bounced off, no doubt leaving a sizable dent. Hilda probably could've threaded a needle with this pod, but Sloane would have to settle for good enough.

Something pinged into the ship from behind, and she accessed the rear cameras to see that Fox Clanners were finally getting their shit together. At least, they were getting it together enough to start shooting at her from doorways.

Fox Clan was famous for installing weapon-mods in

their bodies. Mostly she'd heard about the blades, but a couple of these guys were aiming bare arms at her. Bare arms with gun barrels attached.

Great. That was just great.

"Fortune," Sloane said, "don't tell me you've abandoned me."

"I've never seen a ship like that before," he replied. "I can't even guess where the shield controls would be. Also, I can't *see* you."

That was unfortunate. The pod was tough, but it wouldn't last forever. If the bullets pierced the hull, the atmo wouldn't kill her—Dragon Mother was obviously pressurized—but that would hardly save her from a bullet wound.

Also, she could almost hear the '*that's* your plan?' behind Fotune's words. Though thankfully, he didn't articulate it.

He was trusting her, and so was her crew. She had to win.

Sloane tabbed through her helmet settings until she found a camera. She shared the feed with him.

"All I can see is your face."

She flipped the camera view.

"Better," he said.

"I'll try not to take that as an insult."

"Trouble ahead," he said, but she already saw it: a Fox Clanner with upper arms as big as hams—modded for sure —stood at the far end of the corridor. He looked completely unfazed by the fact that her pod was zooming straight toward him, which made sense, because the guy was hefting a cannon onto his shoulders and aiming it directly at her face.

A shoulder cannon. Interesting. "What'd he do, rip that thing off the outside of the ship?" Sloane asked.

"Yes," Fortune said. He didn't sound like he was joking.

"What do I do?"

"Shoot him."

Crashing into a ship was one thing, but killing someone head-on like that? "I can't *shoot* him."

He hissed out a breath of frustration. "Then duck, because he's going to shoot you."

"Are you serious? That's all you can—"

A second pod rounded the corner ahead of hers, cutting her off from the cannon-wielding Fox Clanner. Plasma fire charged through the corridor, and she didn't have to see the Fox Clanner fall to know he'd fallen.

Heads ducked back into corridors and the shooting tapered off as the second pod took the lead. The very *familiar* second pod. It was, in fact, identical to hers.

"That's my pod, Brighton," Sloane said.

He steered less erratically than she did, centering his ship so it didn't brush the walls, floor, or ceiling. A shame. She suddenly felt the urge to leave as much damage as she possibly could. "You're welcome, kid," Brighton said. "You want to take out those shields, you're going the wrong way. Follow me."

Sloane wanted to ask why he was helping her, but there'd be time for that later. Probably. If they survived. She followed him through the Dragon Mother's lower floors as the ship's crew tried in vain to fight them. Brighton took out each cannon-wielder as they appeared.

Fortune remained silent. Sloane didn't know if Brighton had taken out the comms, or if Fortune wanted to pretend they hadn't been talking—though Brighton had clearly been listening in—or if it was for some other reason that she couldn't guess. Perhaps the Commander had simply been stunned into silence.

It seemed like a year before Brighton changed course abruptly, then crashed straight up through the ceiling, making his own pod-shaped entrance onto the floor above. The room was a treasure trove of tech, with blinky lights and fragile-looking monitors in every corner. Even with the floor in pieces, the tech was mostly intact.

"Shoot it out," Brighton said.

She didn't have to. Not when she had a pod to crash into the walls. Brighton dropped his ship back through the hole in the floor, apparently happy to let her do the destroying.

Good. She was happy to do it.

When the room was in shambles, with fires burning in three separate control boxes, Fortune confirmed that the shields were down. Sloane followed Brighton back through the floor, half expecting him to be long gone, but he was waiting in the corridor below. He ushered her back through the ship—she could have followed the destruction, but it was good to have backup to shoot at people—and thankfully, the exit felt much quicker than the entrance had been.

"OK, Fortune," she said when they were free and clear. "You can kill them now."

"I don't kill defenseless ships, Ms. Tarnish. I take them into custody."

Huh. That wasn't what she'd expected. Though maybe she should have; the guy had a whole weapon system built around deactivating ships rather than blowing them up. Had he gone quiet back there because she'd also refrained from shooting? Why would that bother him?

Maybe it didn't bother him at all.

She could spend a year trying to figure the guy out, but

she had other places to be. Her arm was a blaze of pain, and she wanted to get back to the *Moneymaker*. Now that the Fox Clanners were disabled, the pod felt like insufficient protection against the vacuum. It closed around her like a fist.

"Okay, well," she said, "it's been nice, Fortune. I'll see you around."

"I'm out, too." Brighton was just blatantly using their frequency now, as if she'd invited him to the party. "See ya, kid."

The pod—*her* pod—zipped away toward the Current, and unless she decided to shoot the guy after he'd saved her ass, there was nothing she could do to stop him.

CHAPTER 25

GARETH'S SOLDIERS were boarding the Fox Clan ship from one of *Sabre*'s larger shuttles, his pilots setting a net-rimmed perimeter to deactivate any escape attempts. He intended to take prisoners, and he intended to find out exactly where this ship had been hiding. And who had funded it.

Among many other questions he had.

Sloane's pod was meandering back toward *Moneymaker*. From here, it looked no worse for the wear for all the crashing and banging it had done through that ship. The view from her helmet had made his stomach roil, and not because of the motion, but because the guns that had emerged from every doorway could have meant a killing blow. The thought that he could have been watching her death right along with her... He'd hardly been able to keep his eyes on the screen, and yet he hadn't been able to look away, either. As if his presence, or his attention, could somehow save her.

He couldn't recall the last time he'd felt so helpless.

"Well, it's been nice," Sloane said now. "I'll see you around."

"I'm out, too. See ya, kid." That was Brighton, and Gareth very much wanted to know how the man was piggy-backing onto their frequency. It was meant to be a secure one, direct. But then, it was exactly that skill that made the man a fugitive. From many.

"Lager," Gareth said, "redirect a pair of our stunner pilots. Have them restrain Brighton before he reaches the Current."

Lager nodded. "No problem, sir. Should we take him into custody, or should I have the pilots return him to the *Moneymaker*?"

Either course of action would be acceptable. Brighton was a Fleet-Class criminal who needed to stand trial; he was also the subject of a Federation-approved bounty, one that had been posted out of Halorin—which was a reputable System. One that would thank the Fleet and the Federation alike for allowing the criminal to face charges on their own soil.

After today, Gareth might need to sow some goodwill in Halorin System. They ought to thank him for intervening in this situation today, but he suspected they might just as well tip toward the blaming side. Messes tended to prompt accu-sations first, and Halorin hadn't summoned the Fleet. He had come on his own.

Lager was still waiting on an answer, the question hanging between them. Whatever the man was thinking, he should stop it. Immediately.

"No need," Gareth said. "I'll do it myself."

CHAPTER 26

SLOANE HAD MADE a bit of a mess in the Halorin System.

Authorities from the three nearest planets were whirl-winding around uselessly, circling the deactivated Clan ships while the Fleet cleaned up the Dragon Mother situation.

She couldn't help wondering how many times her father had tried to call her in the last hour or three. She was willing to bet he knew exactly what was going on in Halorin, and who was responsible for it.

When Fortune's ship requested access to board *Money-maker*, she left the pod—she'd just been sitting there, reveling in the fact that she was still alive and trying to blink away her dizziness—and went down to meet him at the airlock. She hadn't had time to check cargo, which was also where the airlock fit in, and she had to step carefully over the bits of the crate Brighton had broken during his escape.

If she was going to continue to pick up bounties, she'd need a better brig. Though to be fair, most people weren't as big as Brighton.

She hadn't had time to visit the infirmary either; she

was still holding her arm tightly against her body. At least Hilda had patched the ship's life support, enough for them to take their helmets off. It would make it more comfortable to hobble toward the nearest moon for help. If any place in Halorin would agree to help them.

The airlock cycled, and to her surprise, Fortune ushered Brighton onto *Moneymaker*. Brighton's wrists were locked in a pair of magna-cuffs, and he had the audacity to smile at her as she stepped aside to let him through. "I guess you're going to turn me in," he said.

She studied the big man for a moment, trying to sort through her pain-muddled thoughts. She had what most would view as a very bad idea, but her gut was tugging at her, and she'd learned to follow that. "You can unlock him," she said.

She expected Fortune to argue, but he didn't. Sloane ignored the Commander, for the moment, and stepped up to Brighton. The fugitive stood two heads taller than she was, yet he looked down at her with a sheepish expression that said he wouldn't try anything.

"I was thinking," she said, "that I'd offer you a job."

Brighton blinked. "All right."

At least he had the sense not to argue. "Good. Now go fix the AI you broke."

Brighton went. Now they had a security officer *and* a hacker. Good. That was good.

Once Brighton had made his way up to the next level, Sloane turned to Fortune. He was watching her, his gray eyes unreadable as always. At least, they were unreadable until his gaze dropped to study her arm. "That injury needs immediate attention."

Yes. Yes, it did. "You probably think I should turn Brighton in," she said. "Are you going to take him from me?"

Fortune looked at her for a long moment, like he was seeking as many answers in her eyes as she sought in his. For reasons she couldn't quite articulate, she kept expecting him to take a step closer to her—but he maintained his distance, gripping his gloves in his hand like a pair of shields.

"I haven't seen Brighton," he said finally. "He wasn't on the pod when I intercepted it."

Sloane could only stare at him in disbelief. She hadn't thought the Commander had it in him. Clearly, she'd misjudged matters.

For a heartbeat, she thought he was going to say something more. And for a heartbeat, she considered thanking him for his help. Or saying... something else. Anything else. She wasn't sure what, exactly. Just... something.

But then he turned, gloves in his hands, and headed back for his transport. As if that was that. Not even a goodbye. Well sure, the guy was used to battles. Probably teamed up with a lot of random people.

To him, she was nothing but another contact, a complication more often than not. That should be a good thing. She hardly needed to get any more tangled up with the Fleet than she already was.

"I know I screw things up a lot," Sloane said. "But Brighton's okay. I'm sure of it."

The words tumbled out like a betrayal to herself. She hadn't even known they were back there, let alone that they wanted to spill out of her like a confession. Almost, but not quite, like an apology.

Fortune turned back, pulling his fingers into his glove with careful concentration. "I don't know, Ms. Tarnish," he said, and she thought he was talking about Brighton being okay, until he continued, "you seem exasperatingly capable to me."

Sloane didn't have his ability to mask her reactions, and she was pretty sure that her shock showed on her face. He thought she was *capable*? The man needed to have his head checked.

And yet... and yet, he'd trusted her, and she'd come through. With Brighton's help, sure, but she could take a sliver of credit, maybe, for bringing him in as an ally before the battle.

The fact that Fortune saw that, though... It was unexpected, to say the least.

"Stay out of trouble, if you can," he added. And with that, he ducked back into his transport, leaving her to stare after him. For once, she couldn't even think of anything to say.

———

Sloane wasn't surprised to find Hilda and Alex waiting for her in the kitchen when she got out of the med bay. They'd installed themselves in the U-shaped booth, and the way they were staring at her, the biggest surprise was really that they'd let her visit the med-bay at all before confronting her. Though if they hadn't, she might well have vomited all over them.

Her arm was in a sling now, but the nano-healers were doing their thing, so at least the pain had abated. The elbow was badly broken, and fissures of fractures crackled along the forearm and wrist. It would take weeks to heal, healers or no healers.

Hilda made a space for her at the table, but Sloane used her good arm to lift herself onto the kitchen counter across the way. Hilda nodded, like she'd expected that. Alex sat back in her chair.

They didn't look angry. They just looked... defeated.

"Sloane," Hilda said, "we can't stay on the ship if you take that Federation job. We need to find Vincent, or Alex and I... We can't stay."

Relief loosened her chest, and she laughed. Which jostled her arm, making her wince. "Yeah, I don't think that job's open to me anymore. I just hired Brighton."

Just was a relative term, since that had been several hours ago. But judging by the women's open-mouthed expressions, she guessed he'd barricaded himself in engineering to work on BRO. Or to hide from them. She wouldn't blame him for that, though he would need to mingle with her crew eventually.

Vin's crew. They were still Uncle Vin's crew, not hers. Fortune thought he was alive, and that gave her some hope.

He also thought she was exasperatingly capable. Yes, well, so was he. Not that she would ever be foolish enough to tell him she thought so.

Hilda placed her forearms on the table and studied Sloane. She had dark circles under her eyes, and Sloane thought she might not have slept since the night they'd spent in Obsidian City—and even then, the pilot had been keeping an eye on the ship repairs. "How does that help us?" Hilda asked.

"We need to find Uncle Vin," Sloane said. "And now we've got a hacker with muscles on our team."

You are looking for your uncle, Fortune had said. *And you're going to find him. The next step in that process is to check the controls.*

She'd been looking at this all wrong. She'd been trying to take shortcuts and instead ended up taking the long way around. One adventure after another, one side quest turning into another side quest. Alex and Hilda were right; they had to find Vin.

She had no idea how to do that, or what she was doing. But she could figure it out.

"Brighton's the next step in the process." She shifted, reached into the inside pocket of her jacket with her good hand, and fumbled out Ivy's card. She held it up for Hilda to see. "Plus, I've got a lead."

CHAPTER 27

GARETH HAD BEEN TRYING to reach Alisa since he stepped foot back on *Sabre* after delivering Brighton to Sloane. He didn't know what he was thinking, allowing her to take him, except that... Well, Brighton had watched her back once. Gareth liked to think the man would do it again.

She should still watch him, of course.

Alisa never answered, and she never called him back. He let Lager handle the Halorin cleanup while he collected reports from his ships in Adu, interrupting his work to answer worried calls from Halorin leaders where the Lieutenant's reassurances weren't enough.

Moneymaker left the system for stars knew where, the Fox Clan criminals were dispersed to Halorin and *Sabre*'s brig for prosecution and questioning, and still Alisa didn't answer.

And then came the summons, one he hadn't realized he'd been expecting until the words popped across his eye screen. The Fleet Advisory Commission awaited his attendance, and they expected they would not have to wait long.

Gareth sighed, doing his best to collect himself. He

hadn't slept in days, he couldn't recall his last meal, and now Alisa's silence was plain—she'd been trying to stall, to help him deal with this mess in Halorin before he had to answer to the Commission. Whatever levies she'd been trying to build in his favor had clearly failed.

When he entered the V-Space, he froze.

The room had been rearranged. It had been the same since he'd first accompanied his father here—and well before that, if Dad's stories were accurate, and Gareth knew they were—but now the round table was gone. Someone had replaced it with layered tiers, a clear hierarchy arranged in half-circles before him.

No, not before him. Where in the past he'd faced the representatives from the center of a circle, they'd always stood on the same level with him. Now, they looked down on him from above. He felt as if he were facing a tribunal, rather than a board of supposed allies.

Irritating allies, more often than not, but still. Allies they'd always been. Now, he only recognized about half the faces, and some of those he knew had not even been reps before. Businesspeople, some of them. Traders. A few dignitaries here and there, but it was a decided shift. If he hadn't been summoned by the Commission, he would have thought he was facing an entirely different body.

At the center of the room, of course, sat Osmond Clay.

"What is this?" Gareth asked, not bothering to hide his disapproval. There were times to be implacable, and there were times to show your power. He had a feeling the latter was about to become distinctly more important.

"Commander," Clay said. "Took your time, did you?"

Gareth scanned the room. "Where's Representative March?"

Clay folded his hands on the table before him. "Restructuring was in order, Commander. I'm in charge now."

Of an organization that had never *had* a formal leader, that had originally been formed with a mission to advise and protect. It was the core of the Commission, their central reason for being, and yet not one of the other representatives even had the grace to flinch.

No doubt they were in Clay's pocket or facing the barrel of his guns. Every one of them.

"Clearly." Gareth couldn't quite manage to keep the bite out of his tone, but it didn't really matter. Whatever game Clay was playing, it had now moved well beyond Gareth's political range. "I suppose you want a report on Halorin."

"We've received our reports on Halorin already." Clay's smile was ugly. A venomous snake, playing with its prey. "We'll deal with your choice to ignore former Representative March's order to return to Adu next."

Former Representative. Excellent. "The Commission doesn't give orders," Gareth said, but he heard his mistake before the words were even out of his mouth.

Clay's smile widened. "I think you'll find, Commander, that we do now."

THE END

———

Thank you for reading!

Bounty War, the next installment in the Parse Galaxy series, will be available in July 2022. Pre-order your copy today: books2read.com/bounty-war

JOIN THE LIST!

Dying to know where Sloane got her rep for crawling through through plasma cannons? Join my newsletter list to read about it (and Sloane's first meeting with Brighton) in "Highly Irregular," an exclusive *Parse Galaxy* story! You'll also get access to my VIP library, which has lots of other free stuff to read.

Sign up here: https://katesheeranswed.com/highly-irregular/

A NOTE ON THE EXPANDED PARSE UNIVERSE

Yes, Sloane did bring coffee back from the Milky Way.

Sloane, Alex, and Hilda all appear in my superhero series, the *League of Independent Operatives*. I hope it's clear that you don't need to have read those books to enjoy the *Parse Galaxy* series, which stands completely on its own.

But since the events of the *LIO* series take place before the events of this story, Sloane's still working through some of the stuff that happened to her there. References are bound to happen.

It's part of what I'm currently calling the Expanded Parse Universe, or the Parse Galaxy on Earth. I'm working on it :)

The *League of Independent Operatives* is a complete five-book series that follows a women-led team of superheroes. Sloane and her friends don't show up until book two, but if you'd like to sample the series, the first book is currently available for free. You can find it here: books2read.com/alterego

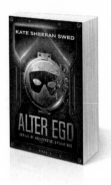

HEIRESS

The world knows Mary O'Sullivan as a Page Six regular; she's an heiress, a playgirl, a philanthropist—and an orphan, after she survived the plane crash that killed her celebrity parents.

The world knows her vigilante alter ego, too—they just don't know it's Mary behind the mask.

OFFICER

Nathan Pearce just wants to be a hero. So when a world-famous vigilante blows through his local Boston bar, he's determined to chase her down. If superheroes do internships, he wants one.

But the woman might as well be a phantom. And Nathan's quest to prove himself will endanger more lives than just his own.

LEADER

Eloise Reyna wasn't meant to inherit a super-secret league

of vigilantes, or the heirloom that grants her powers, for at least another decade. Between her motley band of cranky heroes and abilities she barely understands, she just might lose control.

With a mad scientist on the loose and powerful enemies lurking in the wings, that's simply not an option.

TEAM

Together with their questionable crew, these would-be heroes must untangle the past to secure the future—or allow a dangerous new world order to rise.

The *League of Independent Operatives* is a twisty superhero saga, perfect for fans of *Watchmen*, *Umbrella Academy*, and *Renegades*.

Get your copy of Alter Ego here: books2read.com/alterego

ABOUT THE AUTHOR

Kate Sheeran Swed loves hot chocolate, plastic dinosaurs, and airplane tickets. She has trekked along the Inca Trail to Macchu Picchu, hiked on the Mýrdalsjökull glacier in Iceland, and climbed the ruins of Masada to watch the sunrise over the Dead Sea. Kate currently lives in New York's capital region with her husband and two kids, plus a pair of cats who were named after movie dogs (Benji and Beethoven). She holds an MFA in Fiction from Pacific University.

You can find more of Kate's work, and pick up a free novella, at katesheeranswed.com.

facebook.com/katesheeranswed

instagram.com/katesheeranswed

ALSO BY KATE SHEERAN SWED

PARSE GALAXY (A BRAND NEW SPACE OPERA SERIES)

Outlaw Rising (A Parse Galaxy Prequel Novella)

Chaos Zone

Bounty War - *coming July 26, 2022!*

LEAGUE OF INDEPENDENT OPERATIVES (SERIES COMPLETE)

Alter Ego

Anti-Hero

Mastermind

Nemesis

Defender

TOCCATA SYSTEM NOVELLA TRILOGY (SERIES COMPLETE)

Parting Shadows

Phantom Song

Prodigal Storm

Complete Trilogy Box Set

STORY COLLECTIONS

Don't Look Back (And Other Stories)

Remain Alert: Science Fiction Stories

For information on my other work, including my young adult titles, visit katesheeranswed.com.

Made in United States
North Haven, CT
07 May 2022

18977523R00131